An Ordinary Courage
NAOMI IN INDONESIA

An Ordinary Courage
NAOMI IN INDONESIA

By Karmel Schreyer

GREAT PLAINS FICTION

Great Plains Publications
420 – 70 Arthur Street
Winnipeg, MB R3B 1G7
www.greatplains.mb.ca

Great Plains Publications gratefully acknowledges the financial support provided for its publishing program by the Government of Canada through the Book Publishing Industry Development Program (BPIDP); the Canada Council for the Arts; as well as the Manitoba Department of Culture, Heritage and Tourism; and the Manitoba Arts Council.

Design & Typography by Relish Design Studio Inc.
Printed in Canada by Friesens Printing

CANADIAN CATALOGUING IN PUBLICATION DATA

Main entry under title:

Schreyer, Karmel, 1964-

 An ordinary courage : Naomi in Indonesia / Karmel Schreyer.

ISBN-10: 1-894283-70-8

ISBN-13: 978-1-894283-70-0

 1. Indonesia—Juvenile fiction. I. Title.

PS8587.C487073   2006   jC813'.54   C2006-903941-0

For Frieda, Vera, Fista and Ferdi,
and Mr. and Mrs. R, with gratitude.

—Karmel

JAKARTA

BALI

LOMBOK

INDONESIA

Dear Reader,

This story is set in Indonesia, but the problems and events described herein have happened, and continue to happen, all over the world. They have become part of our global experience. Some of the events will be familiar to you; some you will soon be learning about. I have altered the chronology of actual events for this story, and invented other events, as well as characters.

This story is a work of fiction. But the spirit of those who have lived through such events, and the inspiration they offer us, is very real.

I hope you will enjoy the story of a young girl who discovers her courage— the courage in all of us.

—Karmel Schreyer, Hong Kong, 2006

I have been longing to make the acquaintance of a "modern girl," that proud, independent girl who has all my sympathy! She who, happy and self-reliant, lightly and alertly steps her way through life, full of enthusiasm and warm feelings; working not only for her own well-being and happiness, but for the greater good of humanity as a whole.

—*Raden Adjeng Kartini*

1

satu

September 11: Jakarta, Indonesia (on the island of Java).

…It's funny how life goes. How things happen the way they do. It's pretty incredible and awesome if you think about it, really. Just a month ago, I was getting ready to live the life of a university student, studying business administration at McGill University. Getting ready to live life on my own in Montreal. And now I'm not. I'm here instead, with Mom and Dad and Mei-mei—in INDONESIA! Life is a thrill. An unexpected thrill. How can anyone sleep when they are teetering on the brink of a new adventure—a whole new life?

NAOMI PUT DOWN HER PEN AND BEGAN TO READ. "I can't," she whispered, when she came to the end of the passage.

Naomi closed her journal and got up from the sofa where she had been stretched out, writing her thoughts. The adjoining room, where her mother, stepfather, and sister were sleeping, remained quiet. She looked at the television and saw a familiar face on CNN; Naomi had muted the television so her jet-lagged family would not be disturbed. She stood in the centre of the room and held her head still. Through the hotel's sealed windows, she could barely hear the faint ambient noise from the city's busy streets below. Naomi felt a tingle in her body, and in her mind. A new adventure. A big new city. A huge new country to explore and to understand—and this was *the moment.* The moment it would all begin. *I'm in Indonesia*, Naomi thought. *With Mom and Dad and Mei-mei.* She knew there was more than a little relief mixed in with her feelings of excitement, but she wasn't about to admit that to anyone. Her relief at staying with her family—at her reprieve from living life on her own—was going to be her secret, and one that she was not going to spend too much time thinking about, she had decided. Instead, Naomi was focused on the excitement a new adventure always brought to her, along with the joy and security of experiencing it with her family.

Naomi stood, thinking back to the other moments in her life when she had felt this same kind of nervous excitement. *I remember feeling this way when Mom and I were in Japan. I felt it two years later when Mom and I arrived in Hong Kong*, she thought. That had been almost three years ago, but in some ways it seemed much further back in her life. So much had happened since then. Naomi's mother had married a wonderful man, Naomi's stepfather, Steve, and together the three of them adopted a baby girl from China.

Naomi recalled the first memory of her little sister; an image of a serious, dark-eyed baby sitting in a metal cot in a whitewashed room. She and her mother and stepfather had just been told by the house mother at the orphanage that the baby girl had been abandoned in front of a police station in a city in northern China. Naomi began to smile. That first image of her sister was being replaced by an image much more recent: of Mei-mei charming the flight attendants on the plane from Canada earlier in the day. *Mei-mei is not the same person she was back then*, Naomi thought. *I am not the same person I used to be. Hong Kong changed me. It changed us all.*

Naomi walked to the window and opened the curtain. The hotel room was on the top floor, and the lights of the dark city of Jakarta shone below. To Naomi, it was a velvet blanket with a thousand points of light, spreading out as far as she could see. *It certainly looks different from Hong Kong Harbour.* Naomi continued to wander through the memories of her life in Hong Kong; her friends—especially Jovita, her steadfast pal, who wasn't afraid of telling her the truth about anything, even about the possibility—the *probability*—of acquiring a stepfather, when it was the last thing in the world Naomi had wanted. *She was right about that*, Naomi thought. *Steve is the best.* Then Naomi's smile faded and she sighed. Her thoughts turned to another man she had met in Hong Kong. *Chen.* Naomi saw his smiling eyes, and she pictured him talking to her, over tiny cups of jasmine tea, about Taoism and destiny, and so many other fascinating things about China. Naomi pictured Chen as he stood in the small park practising Tai chi, his body old, but strong and steady. Naomi's eyes began to sting. In her mind she saw Chen's face as it appeared in the old photograph that had been printed in the *South China Morning Post*. *Typhoon Hero*—the headline had read in bold letters—*Receives Posthumous Bravery Award.*

The doorbell chimed. Naomi's breath caught and she ran a finger under her eyelids, then moved to her parents' bedroom door and opened it slightly. "Wake up," she stage-whispered. "Dinner's here. How about a cup of coffee you guys?" She crossed the room and opened the door to the corridor. Naomi took in the welcome smell of eggs, bacon, and coffee. She smiled in anticipation, immediately cheered up by its comforting familiarity.

"*Selamat malam,*" she said to the young man as he pushed the room service trolley in front of the television.

The waiter looked at Naomi with a surprised smile. "Good evening," he answered back. "Welcome to Indonesia. You can speak *bahasa Indonesia* very well."

Naomi grimaced as if to disagree, but then nodded at the young man. "*Terima kasih,*" she replied. She gave the waiter a tip and accompanied him to the door.

"I hope you enjoy your visit," the young man said as he turned to leave.

Naomi wanted to tell this young man that she was not a tourist, and that she and her family had just arrived here to stay for a long time. "I know I will," she replied. "We're going to live in Lombok!" Naomi was surprised to hear the pride in her voice, and felt her cheeks getting warm with embarrassment.

The waiter turned back and grinned. It was a wide grin, showing his surprise and delight at what he had just been told. "Lombok!" he said. "You are lucky, Miss. I wish you well."

"Thank you. *Terima kasih!*" Naomi replied. She accepted the buoyant happiness she felt at that moment as a good sign. *Yes, I am lucky.*

Naomi poured herself a cup of coffee, then looked around the dim hotel suite, lit by the lamps at both sides of the sofa. She moved to the window, looked out again at the glittering city of Jakarta, and raised her coffee cup. "Good evening, Indonesia," she said to the city. "Or is it morning? It feels like morning. It even smells like morning." Suddenly a small, self-conscious giggle erupted from her throat. "I'm going to have some java ... in Java—"

"*Naomi akan minum kopi*. Naomi will drink coffee. That sounds like a good idea," said Sara, as she stepped groggily from the adjoining bedroom, and Naomi turned at the sound of her mother's voice. "I shouldn't have let myself lie down. I've been asleep for three hours! And now, it's almost time to go to bed." Sara shook her head in exasperation.

"*Steve mau minum kopi*. Steve wants to drink coffee," said the man who was following Naomi's mother into the room. He joined his wife and stepdaughter at the trolley and poured himself a cup. "Java in Java," he laughed. "Does that mean we'll have to eat turkey in Turkey someday?"

"Or ice cream in Iceland," added Naomi, as they moved to the window.

"That's stretching it, Naomi," said her mother, grinning, as she brought the cup to her lips.

Naomi giggled. "Hah! Nanaimo bars!"

"What are they?" asked Steve.

"Poor you," said Naomi. "Only Canada's best gooey treat. You're part Canadian now, so you'd better know these things."

"And let me guess. They're from...Nanaimo? Where's that?" Steve pointed to the assortment of maps of Indonesia that were spread out on the floor next to the sofa. "You're my walking world map, Naomi...can you give me a hint?"

Naomi rolled her eyes at Steve, trying hard not to laugh. There was a moment of silence as they stood together at the window, sipping their coffee. Steve was about to say something when the sounds of a waking child interrupted his thoughts.

"Something tells me it's going to be a long night," said Sara as she put down her cup. "Who knows when she'll fall asleep again? I'll get her."

Steve and Naomi smiled at each other as Sara headed to the bedroom to retrieve Mei-mei.

"It's funny how cities look different, even at night, when all you can see are the lights," said Steve.

"That's true," Naomi agreed. "I don't suppose any city is as lovely as Hong Kong at night. All those lights…and the water. It's so beautiful from the harbour."

"You could be right," answered Steve. "But every city—every country—has its own special something."

"I think so, too," Naomi replied. "I can't wait to find out what that's going to be for us *this* time—"

"Here she is, our sleepyhead…one hopes," said Sara in a lilting voice as she brought Mei-mei into the room. Sara reached for a piece of toast from the trolley, passed it to the little girl, and then set her down on the carpet.

Naomi's eyes lit up and she turned to Steve. "I know! Chicken Kiev in Kiev!"

"Good one," answered Steve, still in the game. "Yorkshire pudding—"

"In Yorkshire!" Steve and Naomi said together. They laughed, thinking about Steve's home of Yorkshire, in England's north country.

"What?" whispered Sara.

"Yorkshire pudding—" Naomi began. She looked over at her mother and her smile disappeared. Sara was looking at the television, her face a picture of bewilderment.

"What?" Sara repeated, louder this time.

Naomi and Steve followed Sara's gaze. The room was silent but for Mei-mei's contented munching. Naomi looked, but could not understand what she was seeing. "Mom?" she said, almost in a whisper. "What is—that?"

They were looking at the twin towers of the World Trade Center, the famed landmark of Manhattan. Thick black smoke was billowing out from one of the skyscrapers. Steve reached for the television remote control and switched on the sound.

"…it may be that this is some kind of air traffic control accident…"

Naomi listened to the quavering voice from the television, and felt alarmed by the confusion she heard in the man's voice.

"What on earth?" Steve said.

"What's he saying?" Naomi asked, turning to Steve.

Naomi watched Steve move forward to pick Mei-mei off the floor and bring her to him in a protective gesture. The child began to amuse herself with his watch, oblivious to the scene that was unfolding. At that moment, the television showed a large jet glide gracefully into the second tower. A pop, a roar, an explosion; debris and a fireball above the streets of New York City, then, later, screams of horror and disbelief from stricken bystanders. Nothing was making any sense.

"...another plane has just hit the second tower—"

"Oh my God!" Sara cried out.

Naomi sat down on the sofa beside Steve and swallowed hard. She watched in disbelief as another news announcer, reporting from New Jersey and with the familiar Manhattan skyline as a backdrop, looked behind him and then turned back to face the camera. He was uncharacteristically mute, at a loss for words to explain what was going on across the river.

"What's happening?" Naomi asked no one in particular, although she hoped someone would appear on the television and explain the horror they were witnessing. "Dad?" Naomi looked up at Steve. She knew her father did not have the answer, but she needed to ask. Steve looked at her, shook his head slowly, then took her hand and held it firmly. Naomi had never seen that look in his eyes before, and in instant she understood what it was: he felt as confused as she did. Naomi began to understand that, among her feelings of fear and confusion, she felt shocked and helpless, too, and this realization made her more frightened than ever.

"...the people of New York City are under attack..." Naomi watched the city's mayor, Rudy Giuliani, say.

Several hours later, in the middle of the Indonesian night, they were still watching the television news. Sara and Naomi sat together on the sofa, Sara with an arm draped over her older daughter's shoulders. Steve was on the floor, absently playing a card game with Mei-mei, and making sure the young girl was facing away from the television screen. The World Trade Center in New York City no longer existed, and thousands of people, who had been going about their lives just as they did on any other weekday morning, were now dead.

It was dawn by the time Naomi and her parents went to sleep, no better able to understand the catastrophe that was unfolding in New York City. By then, the finger of blame was starting to point in the direction of Muslim extremists. Fear gripped Naomi's heart when this speculation sunk in. As Naomi kissed her parents on her way to bed, they said nothing to each other. Naomi knew they were all thinking the same thing: Muslim extremists were being blamed for the world's deadliest terrorist attack—and they had just arrived to begin a new life in Indonesia, the largest Muslim country in the world.

2

dua

September 13: Jakarta, Indonesia.

Mom asked me if I wanted to change my mind again and go back to Canada for university. She thinks it'll be safer over there. But maybe terrorists will target the CN Tower. Who knows where they'll strike next? I don't want to go back by myself. Especially now. I told Mom I still want to have a year off before I go to university, but I'm not sure what I should do. I feel afraid. I think I'm afraid of being alone. I think I'm afraid of Muslims. It's funny but I don't think I ever met one until I came here. And I feel really sad, too, ever since what happened in New York City. Everybody's just walking around, really sad...

"I THINK NAOMI SHOULD GO BACK TO CANADA. She can still get into McGill. It's not too late, Steve—"

"Didn't you talk to her about that already? I thought she still wanted to have a year out. Don't you think everyone should have a year out, Sara? I did…and I was under the impression that you did, too."

"Yes, I know, but now…I don't know. Naomi says she wants to stay. But I could pull rank…" Sara's voice trailed off.

"Well, Sara, it's not too late for *all* of us to get out of here—if that's what you're thinking—"

"No, Steve, that's not necessary. We will stay. We can't turn down this opportunity—your chance to work for the *United Nations*. I know how important this is for you. But Naomi had been planning to go to university in the first place anyway, remember? I was glad when she changed her mind and decided to come with us, but maybe, under the circumstances, we need to rethink this—"

"If you're worried about our safety here in Indonesia, Sara, because of what the terrorists did in New York City, then we are going to leave here together. I can find a job somewhere else—"

"No. It's not that—"

"Sara, I think it is. What else could it be?"

Naomi was holding her breath as she listened to her parents' hushed conversation, and she could feel how their whispered words reflected her own anxiety. The door to her parents' room was ajar and, as Naomi peered in, she could see them huddled over Mei-mei's cot by the curtained window. Naomi felt lost. For two days her mind had been replaying the horrifying images: an airliner flying into a skyscraper; the World Trade Center towers crashing to the ground; volcanic explosions of debris: the terrified people. The same questions had been crowding her thoughts: *If Muslims are responsible, is this some sort of vendetta against non-Muslims, or against the West and all who represent it? Why do they hate us so much? Would they do it again? Are we safe here?*

Tomorrow Naomi and her family were going to leave Jakarta and move to their new home on the island of Lombok, right next to the world-renowned tropical island paradise of Bali. The excitement Naomi had felt on arrival was gone; it had vanished as she stood watching a jetliner glide into a New York skyscraper on television and it wasn't going to come back. Naomi felt bereft; the adventure that she had been looking forward to for so long had seemed to no longer exist. Now, just like her mother, Naomi wondered if staying in Indonesia was the right thing to do. She had even thought, with a sense of relief, that her mother might insist they leave— but *all* of them, together, as a family. Naomi wasn't sure if she wanted to stay, but she knew she didn't want to return home by herself. And now, Naomi felt indignantly, here was her mother trying to convince Steve they should send her back to Canada—*alone*. Impulsively, Naomi burst into the bedroom.

"And if I go to McGill…who's to say they won't try something there? Montreal is close enough to New York—"

Naomi's parents turned, startled. Mei-mei began to stir.

"Sweetheart. I'm sorry you heard that. You shouldn't have been standing there, listening—" Sara began.

"Yeah, well… you want to get rid of me, because you're scared. But you're not even thinking of leaving here yourself—"

"I'm not that scared," replied Sara wearily. "I don't think we need to be paranoid about being here. It's not like *The Year of Living Dangerously*, or anything like that."

Steve smiled slightly at his wife's remark. "You don't think so?" he said, trying to defuse what was becoming a tense situation, especially if it meant that Mei-mei would be woken up. This was something he'd discovered he was good at doing, when it was called for, which wasn't that often. He gave his wife a gentle hug. "I kind of thought it was like that—coming here to live, under these new circumstances. In some sort of crazy…very, very sad…way." He smiled wanly at his wife.

Sara looked up at her husband and smiled back, appreciating her husband's effort to smooth things over. She rested her head on Steve's shoulder, and he kissed the top of her head before turning his attention to his daughter. "Come on, Naomi. We'll talk in the other room," he whispered, before leading Sara and Naomi out of the bedroom. Naomi frowned, wondering what her parents had just been referring to. *What did they mean: The year of living dangerously?*

"Sara," Steve said. "I think we need to listen to Naomi on this. We can't be planning her life for her. She's a big girl now—" His eyes met Naomi's as he was speaking, and she could see the familiar twinkle in his eyes as he smiled at her. Something in Naomi jerked back to life. *That smile is so much a part of him—even now*—Naomi thought. *Even still, when the world has just turned upside down.* Naomi felt grateful for Steve's strength.

"But—" Sara began. She looked ready to launch into an argument, and then, just as suddenly, a look of resignation settled over her face, and heavily on her shoulders, too. Sara looked from Naomi to Steve, and took a deep breath. "I think—you may be right." Sara turned back to her daughter, as if studying a face she could hardly recognize. A wistful smile spread across her lips. "It's hard for a mom to admit it, but Steve's right. You're old enough to start making your own big decisions, Naomi." After a pause she added, "So don't hold that conversation you just heard against me, okay?" Sara looked down at her hands for a moment, then up again at Naomi. "But understand this. I would do anything to protect you. I don't know—nobody knows—how safe this place is, but Indonesia already has its fair share of problems. Civil unrest and things like that. This Muslim extremism has just added to it. Do you understand why I'd feel so much better if you went back to Canada now, and stuck to our original plan?"

"Yes, Mom, I do," Naomi replied. "Montreal seems like a safer place. But like you said, do we really know how safe *anywhere* is? New York City was safe enough, until—"

Sara nodded. "Yes, you're right."

"So if you're *that* worried, why wouldn't you want to go back yourself?" Naomi asked, determined to understand her mother's thinking.

Sara smiled self-consciously. "I see, Naomi. It may sound to you like I'm not making any sense. Or being selective in my principles. But some of us have to carry on, despite..." she waved her hand, a little impatiently. "I mean—sometimes we just have to put one foot in front of the other and *keep going.* What I mean is—people—with things to do. People with jobs. I guess," she finished weakly. She huffed, and Naomi knew her mother was annoyed for not being able to better explain what she was thinking.

Naomi realized that her mother was exhausted. *She was probably up all night*—worrying about us. Naomi decided to try to make light of things, the way Steve could. She managed to laugh a little with her response, "Mom, that is being selective. Besides, how bored do you think I would be back in Montreal if you were all here—*living dangerously?*"

Sara's eyes grew wide, then she wrinkled her nose and shook her head at her daughter, and put her arm over Naomi's shoulder. "Never mind. Steve is right. This is *your* life," Sara said. She looked down at the floor and spoke softly, as if she didn't quite want to believe it.

"So," said Steve. "The choice is yours, Naomi. What will it be?"

Naomi looked at Steve. *Thanks for believing in me, and for helping Mom believe in me, too.* She took a deep breath and glanced around the hotel room. Her gaze rested at the window. She hadn't gone to it yesterday, to look out over the city, as she had done so eagerly the night she arrived in Jakarta. For a moment Naomi wondered if she had been afraid to. But now, Naomi felt that things were becoming clearer. Naomi was looking out at a new and unfamiliar view: in the light of day, Indonesia had become another whole new world—another version of the adventure she had been hoping for. Even if the whole world had changed two days ago, maybe that adventure would still be there. Naomi wasn't totally sure about this, but the idea made her feel a little less fearful.

"I'm staying with you."

•　•　•　•　•　•

Naomi sat on the beach near her new home, looking west towards the island of Bali as the sun began to set behind it. It had been several long, exhausting days; getting things moved into their new house in the town of Senggigi, meeting Steve's colleagues from the United Nations Development Program detachment in Mataram, the capital city of Lombok, and all the while making sure Mei-mei was taken care of. They had even made a visit to the site of the water sanitation project where Steve was going to be working for the next two years, and perhaps—if they all decided they liked Indonesia—even longer.

But despite all the non-stop activity since arriving in Lombok three days before, Naomi was already feeling the relaxing effects of living in a sleepy tropical paradise. She took a deep breath and let it out slowly, the way Chen had taught her to do in Hong Kong when she was learning Tai chi. The sprawling, bustling city of Jakarta was already feeling very far away, and Naomi decided that the fearful, anxious feelings she had had back there were not going to follow her to this peaceful place.

Through the mists of the ocean channel that separated Bali from her own island of Lombok, Naomi could make out the dark peaked outline of Gunung Agung against the clear sky. *The most striking thing,* she thought, *is the symmetry of it. To find something so perfectly shaped in nature—it hardly seems possible.* The girl smiled with satisfaction and pride; she had seen that kind of awesome perfection before, when she lived in Japan. She had seen it in Fuji-san, a long-dormant volcano, the tallest mountain in Japan, and that country's most beloved natural treasure. Naomi knew that, to the Balinese, Gunung Agung was just as special, and she smiled at the volcano, pleased to be living so close to another sacred place.

Staring at the volcano in front of her brought Naomi's memories of Fuji back to life. She pictured herself climbing that mountain with her mother when she was twelve. She could feel her laboured breathing, how her throat burned with every breath, how her chest pounded. She remembered the old Japanese man with his granddaughter, whom she was surprised to see so high up on the slope, and how they smiled their encouragement to her. Then Chen's smiling face flashed across her mind once again.

It's nice how you can bring them back—just by thinking about them, Naomi thought. She had often thought about this idea, ever since Chen's funeral; that those you loved—or even those who you may have never known but, in some way, touched your life—could live within you. It was a comforting thought.

Naomi blinked back a tear and stood up slowly to watch the sun disappear behind the volcano, its blue outline now in stark contrast to the orange-pink sky behind it. She headed back to her home, and focused on sounds; the endless rolling waves, dry palm fronds crackling on the ground beneath her feet. As she entered the back garden of her home, Naomi took one last look behind her, at the beach lined by palm trees, the sea, and Gunung Agung standing ageless in the distance. Naomi held her breath. It was beauty beyond description. And even more unbelievably, she could now call it her own.

Back in the house, Naomi was instantly reminded that there was still a lot of work to do. She poked her head in the bathroom to say hello to Steve and her mother, who were giving Mei-mei a bath, then headed to her bedroom. She sat down on the floor by her bed, and began slowly to put some books in the empty space under the bedside table. There was a lot of unpacking left; Naomi had promised to unpack the living room boxes and organize Mei-mei's bedroom. She began stacking a box full of books without looking at them, shoving them on the shelf, their spines jumbled back to front. Naomi couldn't concentrate on the task at hand. She was trying to sort something out in her mind; the beauty and the pain. The pain she had been feeling, and the beauty she had been seeing—all around her at the same time. It felt confusing.

Steve's head popped in from behind the door, followed by his lanky arm and a parcel in his hand. "Naomi. You've got mail," intoned Steve in a familiar way. "Looks like Jovita sent you a care package already."

Naomi jumped up on her knees and reached for the package in Steve's hand. "Mail!" she shouted gleefully, as she ripped off the wrapping and pulled out a DVD. A letter wafted to the ground and Naomi lunged for it:

Dear Naomi,

I found this old movie about Indonesia. It won an Academy Award, I think, back when Mel Gibson was hot. I even watched it before sending it to you. Are you sure you're doing the right thing, going to Indonesia? Just kidding. I would love to come and visit you. Maybe I'll come for Christmas if you can convince me that Lombok is the most beautiful place on earth. That shouldn't be too hard, with Bali so close! My parents love that place. Let me know when I can email you.

Love, Jovita

Naomi looked at the DVD cover in her hand and her eyebrows shot up: *The Year of Living Dangerously.* The coincidence did not surprise her. She was going to find out what Steve and her mother were talking about back in the hotel room in Jakarta after all. But the way Jovita had put it told Naomi that she wasn't going to be reassured by the plot. Jovita had only been joking, but Naomi had decided that living dangerously was nothing to joke about. For her, it was becoming a little too real—and a little too close to home.

3

tiga

Muslims pray five times a day. I read that "Allah u Akbar" (God is Great) may be the most commonly spoken phrase on earth. Ever since I arrived, I've been wondering what I hear from the mosque towers. Wahab told me that, in the morning, they're saying: "God is great. I witness there is but one God. I witness that Muhammed is the Messenger of God. Come to prayer. Come to success. Prayer is better than sleep. God is great. There is but one God." They say it in Arabic.

"ALLAH U AKBAR… ALLAH U AKBAR…" intoned the muezzin.

Naomi drifted awake. She didn't need to look at her alarm clock; the melancholy refrain told her it was 4:30 in the morning. She rolled over, listening to the faint sound of waves on the shore, and the call to prayer from the mosque down the road. Ever since her arrival on Lombok two weeks ago, Naomi had listened to these foreign words, not knowing what they meant. But Steve's colleague, Wahab, had told her last night, and now, as she listened, Naomi smiled with understanding: *God is Great…Come to prayer…God is great.* Naomi knew that Muslims were getting up from their beds in the darkness to pray.

Naomi tried to imagine what it looked like to pray the Muslim way, and wondered what Wahab's family and her Muslim neighbours would be doing at this moment. She thought of the brief newsclips she'd seen on television, of rows of men kneeling and bowing their heads to the floor, side-by-side, inside mosques. *Do they go back to bed after this, or do they start their days now? What do the women and children do?* Naomi could hear another muezzin begin his call to prayer, from a mosque farther away, echoing and overlapping the first in a haunting harmony. *Do they speak only in Arabic? Or do they call to prayer in bahasa Indonesia, too?* Then, as gently as she had been awakened, Naomi was lulled back to sleep by the sounds—strange and new, and yet comforting to her ears.

Naomi was woken up a second time that morning when she sensed a presence at her side. She opened one eye to see Mei-mei's face only inches away. The girl's dark, almond eyes had been uncharacteristically somber since their arrival in Senggigi. The family had wondered if Mei-mei's usual playfulness was absent due to the move and all its attendant changes, or because of everyone's dispiritedness since the attack in New York City. Naomi, Steve, and Sara had talked about it, and were doing their best to act cheerful for Mei-mei's benefit. They pick up on everything, Naomi remembered her mother saying, meaning that even very young children can sense things going on beneath the surface.

"Good morning, Mei-mei," Naomi said as she pulled her sister on top of her. The little girl smiled happily and wrapped her small arms around her big sister.

"Let's go," said Mei-mei after a planting a big kiss on her sister's face. She rolled off Naomi, back onto the floor, and grabbed her sister's arm.

"Okay, Mei-mei. Just let me get dressed." Naomi pulled on her shorts, tucked in the T-shirt she had worn to bed, and threw a shirt on over it. "Where are we going?" She looked out the window. The sky was light, but the neighbourhood was in shadow. Naomi knew it wasn't until about nine o'clock in the morning that the sun made its way over Mount Rinjani, Lombok's volcanic peak, sending sunshine their way. Naomi glanced at the clock. It was only seven thirty in the morning! "What are you doing up so early?"

Mei-mei pointed to the window and looked at Naomi with an expression that was both stern and sweet. "Let's go to the beach. Please. I want to look for shells."

Naomi looked out the window at the row of palms and the beach beyond. *It's going to be another beautiful day in paradise.* She looked down at her sister and grinned. "Good idea!" she whispered. After grabbing a couple of bananas and a bottle of water from the kitchen, the girls slipped on their sandals at the back door and then shut it quietly behind them. Within minutes they were seated by the water's edge digging trenches in the sand. The sun, still quite low in the east, shone down on Bali's volcano across the strait.

"Mountain," Mei-mei said, following Naomi's gaze and pointing.

Naomi nodded. "Volcano," she corrected gently. "A dormant one, though," she added after a pause, more to herself than to her sister. "But who knows when a volcano will become active again. Mount Merapi, on Java, blew its top just last week." A chill ran through Naomi as she remembered reading on the Internet how hundreds of villagers had to flee for their lives.

Mei-mei stepped up to her sister, with her hands on her hips. "What's you mean?" she asked, and offered up a comical, quizzical look that she knew her older sister would enjoy.

Naomi threw back her head and laughed. "Nothing for you to worry about, my little friend. Let's dig our way to China!"

As the two girls continued making trenches, Naomi's thoughts returned to Mount Merapi, and of the place where she had been reading about it a few days before—the business centre of Senggigi's deluxe resort. Naomi had gone to the hotel to buy some stamps a week ago, and was pleased to find a place where she could read email and browse the Internet. The staff had told here where Senggigi's post office was located, and had teased Naomi for not being able to find it in the town's tiny business district, which was just a fifteen-minute walk from her home. *Although calling Senggigi a town is a bit of a stretch*, Naomi decided. *It's more like a village.*

The main shopping area on the island, with streets of stores, a large farmers' market, and a big new shopping mall, was found in the city of Mataram, about forty-five minutes away by taxi. *Much longer, of course, if you're riding a donkey cart—which is not an unusual occurrence on Lombok,* Naomi thought. She had already been offered lifts on donkey carts several times when she walked into Senggigi town each morning to check her email, and to see what was happening in the world. She had even managed to send messages to Jovita in Hong Kong and her grandparents back in Canada.

As Naomi helped her sister shore up the foundations of a sand castle, she thought back to the first time she had gone to the resort hotel with her mother and sister for a swim in the pool, just days after they had arrived in Lombok. As an employee of the small United Nations contingent stationed on the island, Steve and his family had been given access to the hotel's luxurious facilities, and Naomi quickly guessed that a lot of spouses and children of foreign workers were making use of this employment benefit. Several times Naomi had overheard conversations among women whose husbands worked for multinational companies, and were busy building more resort hotels on both Bali and Lombok. One woman had talked about her husband working on plans to build an international airport on the island, and Naomi had listened carefully to that conversation; Steve had spent many years in Hong Kong working on the construction of the new international airport there.

But it hadn't taken Naomi long to realize she preferred the beach by her home instead, with her unobstructed, personal view of Gunung Agung—and so did Mei-mei. These days Naomi went to the hotel only to look at the Internet and check her email. Usually Naomi was the only customer in the small business centre, but yesterday a young woman had been there. Naomi remembered the young woman's eyes flicking up at her as she had entered. She had lowered her voice slightly as she continued to talk on the phone:

"Dad, things are really great here. I'm really enjoying teaching English. Jakarta's a big city, but there are other places to see...I'm in Lombok now, for a bit of a break...The pay is good. It's great to have some money—finally...I'm going to pay off my student loan first...I'd like to come back for Christmas but it's so expensive...I better go now...I miss you and Mom...I love you, Dad...Bye." When the young woman left the room, Naomi had pretended to be reading the news on the Internet.

Naomi's thoughts lingered over the young woman. *She sounded like this was her first job, her first time away from home. An English teacher...I'll bet she was Canadian.* Naomi was sure of it. She had come across a lot of Canadians teaching English in Asia. Naomi had done it herself as a 12-year-old in Japan, leading a group of kids in a boisterous rendition of Simon Says. Naomi was reminded that she and her mother had been thinking of things to do in Lombok, and that teaching English was an idea at the top of the list of possibilities.

After building a sand castle with a moat, Naomi and Mei-mei waded into the surf to hunt for shells, and were abundantly rewarded in no time. They laid their gifts from the sea out on the sand to dry, then sat to admire the different shapes. Naomi was absorbed in studying nature's faultless design.

"I'm hungry."

Naomi's attention snapped back to the present. Her sister was already standing up, waiting to go. The sun was shining down on them now, hot and still. Naomi stood up, brushed off some sand, and took Mei-mei's hand. As they neared the house, Naomi glanced over to the street and saw a woman walking by, dressed in a long flowing garment, and wearing a white head covering. Naomi looked down at her bare legs again, aware that the Muslim women of Lombok did not dress as she did, and was reminded that her mother was now in the habit of wearing long skirts and ankle-length cotton pants. As they entered the back door, Naomi found her mother and Steve seated at the kitchen table, eating a fruit salad breakfast.

"I saw you out on the beach," said Sara. "How long have you been out there?"

"Since—early," Naomi replied. "Mei-mei was up."

"Kopi?" Steve asked, brandishing the coffee pot.

"Ya, terima kasih," answered Naomi as she sat at the table, plopping Mei-mei in her lap.

The doorbell rang.

"That'll be Wahab and his family," Steve said to Naomi. "I know I'm new here, but I can tell you that man is *brilliant.*" Steve put the coffee pot on the counter and headed to the front door.

Sara beamed. "We've invited them over. We thought it would be nice for the families to get to know each other, since Steve and Wahab will be spending so much time together."

"That's a good idea," replied Naomi. Wahab had mentioned the night before that he had three children, and Naomi was wondering when she would have a chance to meet them. "What exactly does Wahab do, Mom? Is he a civil engineer like Steve?"

"No. He's the local liaison. Steve says Wahab has been his lifeline at work; showing him the ropes, who to see to get things done, introducing him to the other staff and local contractors." Sara went to the cupboard and got out more cups and saucers. "I can't imagine it's going to be easy to build a wastewater treatment plant in a place like Lombok."

Naomi chuckled. "Makes building the largest airport in the world in Hong Kong a piece of cake, maybe?"

Steve came into the kitchen, followed by a smaller man, slightly older, but with smiling eyes and a grin that made him appear youthful. "Wahab's alone this morning, sorry to say," he said. "Wahab, you've already met Sara and Naomi. But this is Mei-mei."

"Good morning," Wahab said, grinning at Sara and Naomi. His smile widened as he reached out to shake Mei-mei's hand. "I'm very pleased to meet you, little girl," he said, trying to appear formal, but the twinkle in his eyes betrayed his delight, and Mei-mei knew it. She smiled up at him as she took his hand.

"Would you like some coffee, Mr. Wayuni?" asked Sara.

"I would. Thank you very much."

"I'm sorry that your family is busy today."

"Actually, I am hoping we can go together into Mataram this morning. My family is expecting us there—"

"Great! It's about time we figured out our way around the island—and not just Senggigi," said Steve, as he motioned for Wahab to take a seat at the kitchen table.

Sara set a cup of coffee in front of Wahab. "That would be lovely. Thank you, Mr. Wayuni. We've been looking forward to meeting your family."

"Please call me Wahab," he replied. "They are eager to meet you, too. We thought that, because today is a national holiday, you might like to see what's going on in the big city."

"What festival are we going to see?" asked Naomi.

Wahab scratched his head. "Well, it is not a festival. On this day, we are reminded of certain events, over 30 years ago, which lead the way for our president to assume power," he looked up at Steve and chuckled. "The armed forces come out on this day. Others, too, in support of his government. It's what you might call…a bit of propaganda. But there is a fair at the marketplace, games of chance for the little ones…My children—my girls—like the excitement," he added. "They think it's like a parade, a festival."

"If there are big crowds in Mataram, how do you suppose we can meet up?" asked Steve.

Wahab looked amused. "Steve. Of course, I will arrange it. I'll call my brother's restaurant in Mataram. My family will meet us there for lunch."

"You make it sound so easy…and all without mobile phones," said Sara.

"It is," Wahab grinned. "I know everyone in Lombok."

At twelve o'clock, the two families were seated around a table in a small but busy restaurant. Naomi quickly spotted Wahab's wife and their three children: two girls who looked to be about 10 years old, and a tall teenage boy.

"Hello Mrs. Wayuni. We are so glad to finally meet you," exclaimed Sara. "I cannot tell you what a help your husband has been to Steve—all of us—since we arrived."

"Oh, please, call me Farah. And I shall call you Sara." Wahab and Steve and Sara laughed together. "We are so happy to meet you and your family, too," Farah said as she reached for Sara's hand.

Immediately, Naomi knew she liked Farah. Her smile and demeanour were as warm as her husband's. The twins, too, Naomi thought, seemed naturally cheerful and friendly, but as she eyed their older brother, it seemed somehow that he didn't belong. She nodded hello, smiling at everyone, her eyes quickly passing over the tall young man standing next to his mother. There was not much of a smile on his face, and Naomi thought she had caught him looking at her legs with the same grim expression. Self-consciously, Naomi slipped her bag off her shoulder and held it in front of her, covering her bare knees. She felt her face go red, and began to wish her mother had suggested she change into trousers or a long skirt. But the thought flew from her mind when she noticed that Mei-mei was staring in confusion at the two young girls standing next to her.

"Yes, my dear, they're twins. This is Jameela and this is Fathima…they're 12 years old," said Farah to the awestruck Mei-mei, then looked up at Naomi and her mother. "And this is our son, Noor. He's a student at Mataram University," she finished proudly.

Noor attempted a smile. To Naomi, he looked unhappy. *Maybe he's shy,* she thought. *Or maybe he just wishes he were out with his friends. It's the weekend, after all.*

While Steve and Wahab talked over the menu with Noor, Naomi listened as her mother's conversation with Farah turned from their husbands' work, to schools for the youngsters. When Sara mentioned about her and Naomi's wish to keep themselves busy during their stay in Lombok, perhaps by teaching English, Farah lit up.

"What a wonderful idea," she said, holding Sara's arm tightly in her excitement. "I am an English teacher—or, I used to be. Languages are so important—I keep telling my children," she continued, glancing up at Noor. "My son is a linguistics student. So, you see, I have tried to have my children learn English well, but it has been a lot of work. Lombok could do with an English school—"

Sara laughed. "Wow…I was thinking of, just, tutoring in our home. I certainly wasn't thinking about setting up a school—"

"Oh, but you must—or you should," Farah said, then added, "I'm sorry my enthusiasm is getting away from me—"

Wahab chuckled. "Yes, Farah, it sounds like you are issuing orders—to my colleague's wife!"

Everyone around the table laughed at Wahab's remark, except for Mei-mei, who didn't understand the joke—and Noor as well, who was taking in the banter with a sullen expression. *Maybe I'm imagining it,* Naomi thought, still wanting to give Noor the benefit of her doubt. She didn't want the truth to be that Noor just didn't like them, for some reason.

After lunch Wahab announced that it was time to find a good place along the route to see the festivities. Steve decided that everyone would ride together in his vehicle and, with Wahab driving, they made their way slowly through the streets of Mataram, which were clogged with an assortment of vehicles, carts, and pedestrians eager to see the spectacle. It took a while to find a parking place, but soon everyone was heading to the main street on foot, looking for a good vantage point. Naomi was holding on to Mei-mei, walking alongside Farah and her mother.

"Your husband said today is like a festival?" Naomi said to Farah, making it sound like a question. Naomi could tell that her mother liked Farah, too, and felt glad that her mother had found a friend so soon.

Farah smiled, and repeated what her husband had said earlier, "It's…well…it's not a real festival—a *fun* thing. It's an important occasion—"

"To show our love for Wirano," interrupted Noor.

Naomi was startled by Noor's unexpected interruption, and also by the sarcasm she detected in his voice. He had been walking behind her and his mother, obviously listening to the conversation. Naomi turned around to acknowledge his comment.

Wahab shot his son a stern glance, then turned to Steve with an apologetic look. "These days, it is more a show of force, rather than a show of national pride," he remarked dryly. "To keep the people in line. Wirano is losing his grip." After a pause, Wahab lowered his voice even further and added, "It's been a long time coming."

Naomi knew that Noor and Wahab were referring to the president, who had been in power for more than 30 years. She had read about him while they were still in Hong Kong, after Steve and her mother had announced that the family would be moving to Lombok. Naomi also had read about the president during mornings at the hotel, browsing Indonesia's main English newspaper, and some Australian newspapers, on the Internet. Naomi saw that Steve had responded to Wahab's ominous assertion with an understanding nod. *Wirano is loosing his grip*, Naomi repeated Wahab's words in her mind. That was what had happened in the movie Jovita had sent.

4

empat

Raden Adjeng Kartini was a Javanese princess whose father broke with tradition to allow her to receive an education. She became a woman hero of modern Indonesia, determined to help others in her country. Educator, politician, journalist, defender of human rights, feminist, and a leader for all her countrymen. Go, Kartini! You go, girl!

NAOMI ENTERED THE KITCHEN, where her mother and Farah were working. Her cheeks were flushed and she was out of breath, having run most of the way from the business centre. She sat down at the table, piled high with books as well as pages of notes that the two women had been writing and discussing. "I've got good news! I know what we can call our school."

"Tell us, Naomi. You look so excited, I can't wait to hear what it's going to be," said Farah, matching Naomi's enthusiasm.

"Well—I mean—if you agree," Naomi replied. She looked at Farah across the table. "I got the idea from your money—"

"My money?" Farah looked confused.

Naomi nodded. "What do you think of—Kartini's School!"

Farah sat back in her seat and clapped her hands. "I think it's a wonderful idea, Naomi. And how clever of you to think of it!"

"Well, you'll both have to fill me in—" said Sara, looking from Naomi to Farah.

Naomi pulled out a chair and sat down next to her mother. "There was a woman named Kartini. Raden Adjeng Kartini. She's the lady on the ten-thousand rupiah note," Naomi began. "I read about her on the

Internet. She lived more than a hundred years ago. When I saw her on the money, I thought she was beautiful. Her name was written next to her picture—in fine print. So I looked her name up on the Internet. Mom—she was a Javanese princess, and wasn't supposed to do much, in those days—you know—but she did a lot for the people here. She helped young girls get an education. And in April, there's Kartini Day, to honour her. She's like—a hero to people here." Naomi turned to look at Farah, who was nodding in agreement.

"She sounds like quite a woman, Naomi. But is it a good name for the school?" asked Sara. There was a mischievous smile on her lips when she added, "Don't forget we'll be letting boys into the school, too."

"I know. But Kartini was a hero to everyone—that's what it said. Even little children are supposed to know all about her—"

"You're right, Naomi. *Hari Kartini* is on April twenty-first, the day of Kartini's birth. I always help organize the festivities at my daughters' school. It's a great day for the children—a real celebration."

"See, Mom? I think it would be a good idea to have a name that the students recognize, and a person they really admire—not like 'Rocky Mountain English School' or 'Big Ben English School,' or something like that," Naomi added, thinking of the English school signs she had seen when she lived in Japan.

"I totally agree with you, Naomi," said Farah. "The story of Kartini has much to do with the idea of being open to foreign languages and cultures. She could speak Dutch when few people could—especially young girls—because they did not have the opportunity. Kartini did what she could to help others have opportunities to learn. She was a dutiful daughter too, but also, in some ways, she was a very modern girl for her time."

Naomi's smile froze, and she stared at Farah. "You mean…Kartini didn't speak English?"

Farah raised her eyebrows. "No, Naomi. I'm quite sure she did not. At that time, Indonesia was still under the rule of the Dutch. Kartini learned Dutch, and wrote letters to her Dutch friends—some have been published."

Naomi looked from Farah to her mother and back, then shrugged. "Doesn't matter," she said. "It's still a good name for our school."

Sara tried to contain her laughter, which erupted with a snort, sending Farah and Naomi into a fit a giggles.

"Okay, then. I'm convinced," said Sara after she had composed herself. "The more I think about opening an English school here in Senggigi, the more excited I get." Sara paused for a moment, then looked up at Farah. "Doing something like this was the last thing I would have imagined, after all that has happened since our arrival in Indonesia."

Farah's grin faded and she sighed. "I know. The talk among many of the foreigners living here in Lombok is that they want to take their families and go home. Some have already. Wahab mentioned that Mrs. Juriks will be taking her children back to Norway, but her husband will finish out his contract. They'll be separated for eight months."

Sara went to the refrigerator and pulled out a jug of pineapple juice. "Well, I wouldn't want to do that. Leave Steve here. I mean…we just got here. I couldn't do it."

"Mom, we talked about this. Terrorists could strike anywhere. Don't be afraid of Indonesia, just because there are a lot of Muslims—" Naomi began.

"Don't be silly, Naomi," Sara replied, a little too sharply.

Farah went to the cupboard and pulled out three glasses. "I wouldn't blame you, Sara. But let me assure you that what these terrorists have done is against everything that my religion stands for. They say they are doing it in the name of Islam, for the love of Allah, but, I'm sure you realize, they are simply terrorists, and nothing more. And, judging by what happened in New York, you may be better off to stay as far away from there as you can…And stay with us," Farah finished, trying hard to put a smile on her thoughts.

"Of course you're right," said Sara. Naomi could see that her mother was trying to brighten up. "I must admit that all this planning for our joint venture is a good way of keeping my spirits up. But I have to tell you that, ever since the attack, I've been—well, I've been sad. Steve said he was, too."

"Me, too," said Naomi. It made her feel better just to say it out loud.

"Me, too," said Farah.

Sara let out a loud breath and blinked hard. "Time for a break. Let's take our drinks and go to the beach, shall we?"

The three headed outdoors and stood facing the sea in silence. Naomi thought about what her mother had said back in the house and realized that she was also grateful for the diversion the school was providing. Being busy helped keep her mind off the tragedy that the world was now calling *Nine Eleven.* Steve and Wahab were supportive of the idea of starting a local English school, pleased that Sara and Naomi and Farah would be in business together.

"Do you remember, Mom, Steve was teasing me by saying that if I could get a language school up and running, I didn't need a university to teach me business administration?"

Sara nodded, then turned to Farah. "Steve said that McGill University's Business School would instead be inviting Naomi to lecture on the finer points of doing business in the Indonesian hinterland. One thing we learned in Hong Kong, is that business savvy is very important, and the ability to make money is a prized skill," Sara explained with a grin.

Naomi smiled at the truth of her mother's statement, but it soon faded. As she stared across the strait, Naomi thoughts were planted firmly in Indonesia. Images and feelings began to flit through her mind in a jumble: the scenes on television at the hotel in Jakarta; her fear and shock; listening in on her parents' conversation about sending her back to Canada—and a myriad of other impressions from that day to the present. Naomi remembered when they had decided, as a family, to continue their Indonesian adventure together, in spite of their fears. And when Naomi and her family flew across the length of Java and over the island of Bali to get to Lombok, Naomi had been fascinated by what she saw: a patchwork of fields, villages nestled among them, trees. Brilliant-emerald. But most unforgettable were the volcanoes; mighty Mount Bromo, the pride of Java, and Mount Merapi too; and the elegant Gunung Agung on Bali.

"I love volcanoes," Naomi stated, eager to change the subject. She pointed across the strait. "And I can't believe *that* is the view from my backyard."

"Well, if you love volcanoes, you've come to the right place," said Farah. "Don't forget Mount Rinjani, Naomi—"

"Yes, so close we can't see it, but we know it's there—towering above us all," added Sara.

Naomi nodded, continuing to reflect on her arrival in Lombok. She had been nervous at first, still wrapped up in the fear that Nine Eleven had brought, still off balance. Watching the movie that Jovita had sent did not quell her unease. It was about the overthrow of the Indonesian president 40 years ago, a tumultuous period in the country's history. Naomi had read about it on the Internet and was horrified to learn that millions of Indonesians had been killed during this time. Before he had been deposed, the president of the day had called the times "the year of living dangerously," but he could not have known how prophetic those words were.

Naomi's thoughts were interrupted by her mother's voice. "You're right, Farah. The beauty of Lombok has won my heart. After Nine Eleven, I wasn't sure if we were doing the right thing by coming here. But there is nothing scary about *this* place—about Lombok. It's just—beautiful here. The rice fields, the mountains, the beach." Sara threw out her arm as she spoke, then let it fall and tilted her head. "You know what I mean?"

"I know *exactly* what you mean, Sara," replied Farah warmly.

Sara continued, as if to try to understand her feelings, "I think, at the time, when we were back in Jakarta, we were just reacting to the tragedy, to what happened in New York City. People were afraid all over the world. Not just here. Not just in Muslim countries. I'm not sure what I think about Muslim life—or Muslim faith. I don't *know* much—*nothing*, really—about it, yet. People who go to extremes, though, that scares me—"

Naomi spoke up. "What I see here, though, the Muslim things, are just so new and fascinating to me. Like the call to prayer." Excitement crept into Naomi's voice. "When I first heard the call to prayer here in Lombok, I had no idea what it was. I had never heard it before. In Jakarta, how can anyone hear anything?" Naomi laughed, and so did her mother and Farah. "That sound—the call to prayer—especially the morning call, when it wakes me up—it feels like music to me."

Sara moved over to her daughter to give her a hug, then looked over at Farah. "It is fascinating for us. The Muslim culture is so different from anything we've ever experienced, Farah."

"I have a wonderful idea!" Farah said. "Naomi, would you like to know more about how we pray?"

Naomi nodded.

Farah had a sparkle in her eye. "Well, then, how would you like to spend the night at our house—with Jameela and Fathima? They will show you what happens during that morning call to prayer that keeps waking you up."

Naomi was surprised by Farah's offer and wasn't about to refuse it; it would answer the question she had been wondering about since her first morning in Lombok. She laughed with excitement. "How did you know, Farah? That was exactly what I was wondering—"

"Every morning, in the dark, at 4:30, right?" Farah giggled. "Come on over tonight, then. Come for dinner, Naomi. When my daughters come home from school I will have to tell them to make sure they clean their room. They will be thrilled to have your company!"

Naomi looked over at her mother, who looked pleased. "That's kind of you, Farah. Such an opportunity. I can't thank you enough—for being—"

Farah and Sara were looking at each other, and in the brief silence, Farah came over to Naomi and her mother and squeezed Sara's arm. "Thank you for being a friend to me, Sara—and now a business partner, too!"

Naomi looked at her fair-haired mother and the dark, exotic-looking woman smiling next to her. She knew her mother was glad for Farah's company. Naomi also felt glad knowing that this woman's husband was Steve's colleague, too. She thought of Jameela and Fathima, who would be Naomi's teachers later in the day. Naomi smiled at the thought of having a slumber party with the two twelve-year-olds; it was something she never would have imagined doing. Mei-mei would be very put out not to be able to tag along tonight, so much did she idolize those identical twin girls. Then Naomi remembered that Noor would likely be there, and her delight dampened slightly. *Noor is not the friendliest of guys, but you can't have everything*, Naomi found herself thinking. *But, maybe, with this family as friends, we've lucked out coming here, after all.*

5

lima

"I'M FINISHED," THE GIRL WHISPERED.

Naomi took back her journal from the girl, who had insisted on writing the answer to Naomi's question in its pages. The girl was taking her mother's instructions to teach Naomi about Islam very seriously, and had woken Naomi up at 4:00 to start her lesson on the morning call to prayer.

Naomi began to read. *Muslim life is based on the Five Pillars of Islam: We believe in one God (we call him Allah) and his prophet, Muhammed. We pray every day. We care about and give to the needy. We fast during Ramadan. We visit Mecca at least once in our life, if we can.*

Naomi looked up and smiled at the girl sitting next to her. "Thank you for explaining all this, and I can't wait for you to tell me more. But, maybe we should turn off the light now. I'm worried that your sister might not appreciate being woken up earlier than necessary."

"Why? It is almost time for her to get up, anyway."

"Is it time?" A voice came from across the room.

Naomi groaned inwardly, feeling guilty. She looked down at the sleepy face staring up at her from the mattress on the floor. There had been a lot of squabbling between Naomi, Jameela, and Fathima the previous evening, to see who would sleep down there. Naomi had been determined not to displace the twin occupants from their double bed, but they would not hear of it. Finally, to be polite, and also so that they could put the issue behind them and get started on some pre-bedtime girl talk, Naomi had relented, and the twins had happily given up their bed for the night.

"Sorry, Fathima—" Naomi began.

"No, I am Jameela."

"Oops," Naomi whispered, flustered and embarrassed. Beside her, Fathima laughed, and Jameela and Naomi joined in. "Sorry for waking you—"

"No. I wake up at this time. It will soon be time for us to pray. Do you want to try?" Jameela said. She reached for the alarm clock on the bedside table. "In seven minutes."

Naomi felt awkward. "I'd like to watch, if that's okay—"

Jameela clambered up on the double bed. "Yes, sure. But mother says we are your teachers. I think you should try—"

Fathima interrupted. "We can teach Naomi to speak our language." She turned back to Naomi. "Can you speak *bahasa*?"

Naomi was charmed by the girls' eagerness, and admitted to herself that she had a lot to learn from these twelve-year-old girls. She felt embarrassed as she shook her head to the girl's question. "No, I can't—"

"Then, we'll teach you. Starting with the numbers—" began Fathima.

"Mei-mei already knows—" said Jameela matter-of-factly, and Naomi almost whooped in surprise. *So that's what Mei-mei had been saying!* She had been wondering what Mei-mei was trying to say to her just a few days before. It had sounded like counting, but Naomi had thought it was some kind of toddler's Cantonese.

"*Satu… Dua… Tiga… Empat… Lima… Enam… Tujuh*—" the twin girls intoned carefully. Naomi felt sure they were saying this no differently than the way they had spoken to her four-year-old sister.

There was a faint crackle of static as the muezzin tested the loudspeaker at the mosque, just a few doors down from the Wayuni home.

Jameela and Fathima immediately stopped their recitation. They got up from the bed and went over to a dresser. Fathima opened the top drawer. Naomi watched as the girls brought out small rugs and carefully placed them on the floor next to the window. Then they returned to the drawer, and donned white headscarves.

"*Jilbab*," said Jameela, pointing to the head covering.

Without a word, the twins went over to their prayer rugs and kneeled. Jameela gave Naomi a sweet smile before she bent down, lowering her forehead to the floor. They were facing the window, and Naomi watched them in the semi-darkness.

"*Allah u Akbar…*" the muezzin said. By now it had become a familiar refrain to Naomi.

At one point, the twin girls sat kneeling with their legs to the side, and Naomi was surprised to see them turn their heads to one side and then the other, as if the girls were touching their chins to each of their shoulders, as they spoke to each other in a language Naomi did not know. Fathima and Jameela appeared focused as they did this, and Naomi wondered if the girls had forgotten that they were being watched. At that moment, when Jameela turned her head one last time, she looked up at Naomi and smiled, she spoke again the unfamiliar words. Naomi smiled back, feeling privileged to be invited to witness this solemn act, but also a little uncomfortable for not understanding what it all meant.

After several more minutes, the call of the muezzin seemed to fade away without any warning. Jameela and Fathima knelt together and bowed, then stood up. They removed their head coverings and returned them to the drawer. Jameela yawned and looked at Naomi and smiled, then, without another word, and much to Naomi's surprise, she lay back down on her mattress on the floor, pulled the sheet up to her chin, and rolled over. Naomi looked at her watch; it was, after all, just 5:00 in the morning.

"Next time, you can try, Naomi," grinned Fathima.

Naomi nodded, and whispered. "Tell me, Fathima, what language is that I hear, when the muezzin speaks. And what did you say to me just then?"

"I said… 'peace,' to you. It's Arabic. I can speak a little of it. Most of us know some," the girl replied. "I can speak English, *bahasa*, and Arabic. What about you?"

"I can speak English, French—and some Japanese."

"Japanese! French! Teach me, Naomi, please?"

Naomi smiled, but shook her head. "How can we have time to do that, when *you* have to teach *me bahasa*—and when we'll *all* be busy teaching English to Senggigi," she said, taking the young girl's hands in hers. They laughed together and then, when the room fell quiet once again, Fathima looked back at her sleeping sister.

She looked up at Naomi. "Good idea," she said, then clambered back into bed on the floor beside her sister. Naomi looked at the two dark-haired girls, thought of her little raven-haired sister, Mei-mei, then smiled and snuggled under her own bedsheet. She lay in the darkness trying to burn indelibly into her mind what she had just seen, trying to make sense of it, understanding only that in ways unknown to her, each movement the girls had been doing was full of meaning. It reminded Naomi of the Japanese tea ceremony, where, also, deep meaning was imbued in every posture, every turn of the wrist. For a moment, Naomi tried to conjure up images of her Japanese "grandmother" Keiko, performing Japanese tea ceremony, and felt disappointed when the images seemed somehow blurred by time. *It seems so long ago…so far away…*

·   ·   ·   ·   ·   ·

"Naomi."

Naomi turned over in bed, and saw the twins looking at her, grinning. She turned to the window, and saw the diffused morning sunlight outside.

"Time for breakfast. Mother asked us to call you."

Naomi jumped up, worried to have kept her hosts waiting. When she finally entered the dining area, the Wayuni family was seated around the table and smiling her way—all except Noor who, once again it seemed, looked up at her askance, his expression unreadable. *"Selamat pagi,"* Naomi said quickly and took her seat at the table next to Wahab. She watched Noor pick up the large plate of bread rolls and offer it to his father.

Wahab smiled and proffered the plate of assorted rolls to their guest, and Farah came over with the coffee pot. She poured her husband a cup and then looked at Naomi. *"Kopi?"* she asked. Naomi nodded gratefully.

"Terima kasih," she said. The twins gigged and clapped, Jameela looked over at her brother. Naomi could see a faint smile on his lips.

"I understand that you got a lesson in morning prayer a little earlier," said Wahab.

"Yes, your daughters were kind to show me what they do. And, I learned something else. I had often wondered what Muslims do after the morning prayer. I wasn't sure if they went back to bed, or what?" Naomi looked at the girls and grinned. "Now I know."

Everyone around the table laughed at that remark, even Noor smiled so wide Naomi could see his teeth. "I see, Naomi. You think we all go back to bed," said Wahab. He chuckled. "To fall back to sleep after the morning prayer, that is to say. But that is not for me, I can assure you."

Farah looked adoringly at her husband. "My husband is one of those devout Muslims who start their day at 4:30 in the morning—"

Wahab laughed heartily. "*Devout* is not really the word, Farah. I just can't fall back to sleep—as you know." His eyes were twinkling at his wife, and Farah put her hand on her husband's shoulder as she poured some more coffee into his cup. He turned back to Naomi. "We are not a strictly devout Muslim family, Naomi. On a scale of one to ten, we are—" he turned to Noor. "What would you say, son?"

Noor looked up, surprised by his father's sudden attention. He looked at his father, whose laughter seemed to put the young man more at ease. Noor shrugged and smiled slightly. "Five…No—four?"

Wahab feigned shock. "Is that all, son? I think we are at least a seven—"

"*Tujuh,*" said Fathima knowingly, taking up the teacher's role again. Naomi started to laugh and almost choked on her roll. Jameela gave her a few thumps on her back.

"Our imam likes to tell us it is devout to stay up after the morning prayer. What every Muslim knows is the saying of our prophet Muhammed: *The most excellent jihad is that for the conquest of self.*"

Naomi nodded, trying to understand what Wahab was telling her. He continued, "It seems that this word has gotten some bad press lately. *Jihad.* Evil people have taken that word and used it to justify their evil actions. But it is a word all Muslims know—" Naomi saw Jameela and Fathima nodding.

"The idea behind that saying is familiar to everyone, regardless of their faith, I think. It simply means that all of us should strive to better ourselves." Farah was smiling as she spoke, but Naomi could sense she was upset.

Naomi nodded. "I understand that."

"Naomi, do you know the saying 'Early to bed, early to rise, makes a man healthy, wealthy, and wise'?" asked Wahab.

"Yes."

"I believe it, too. Our imam suggested that we could do better in our lives if we do not succumb to the temptation of returning to our beds after the morning prayer." He gave his wife an amused glance as he spoke. "Of course, I am not going to tell my young daughters they must be busy at five o'clock in the morning—and we don't expect them to get out of their beds at midnight to do *isha*—the night prayer. As for Noor, he, too, can follow his own lead. But I have always been, how do you say—an early bird. I like to read, for one thing—before my noisy children can distract me. Or sometimes, I will go to the office early."

"I'm an early bird, too, Wahab. We also have an English saying: 'The early bird gets the worm.'"

Wahab looked pleased. He nudged his son and then glanced in Naomi's direction. He laughed. "There you go, Noor, at least one girl who is not lazy, or a pest, like your little sisters." The twins groaned their disapproval at their father's mischievous banter. Naomi thought that Noor was embarrassed by his father's remark.

"Wahab!" said Farah playfully. "Not everyone is as energetic as you."

Wahab blew his wife a kiss, then changed the subject. "You know, Naomi, that the most important time in the Muslim calendar will soon be upon us."

"Ramadan?"

"You're right, Naomi. That means we will have to fast from dawn until sunset every day for a month. This year, my daughters are going to practice *sawm*—the fast—they are now twelve years old. Isn't that right? Pass me another roll, Fathima, please?" Fathima handed her father a roll from her hand. "I know Christians also have a fasting period. It is called Lent, is that right, Naomi?"

"Yes. But I must admit, I've never done it. My mom and I—my family—we're not very religious."

Wahab nodded thoughtfully. "I sometimes wonder if being very religious is such a good idea. Certainly, here in Indonesia religion is a cause for much conflict. We have so many different people living in Indonesia. Different cultures, religions, languages."

"We do, too, in Canada," said Naomi.

"There are sizable Christian communities all over Indonesia," added Farah. "And did you know, Naomi, that Bali is mainly a Hindu enclave?" Naomi's eyes widened in surprise and Farah continued. "It is such an interesting culture, on the island of Bali. The Balinese Hindus came from India hundreds of years ago. I've lived here all my life, and I still find my own country so fascinating." Farah brought a bowl of freshly cut pineapple to the table. "Of course, Lombok is just as interesting as Bali, but not world-famous—"

"I hope it stays that way," interrupted Noor.

"So do I," said Wahab, and Farah and the twins nodded in agreement.

"I've lived here all my life and I am sure I would never want to leave," Farah said. She looked up at her husband. "Wahab, we should all do something this weekend. A trip, somewhere, to show Naomi and her family the beauty of Lombok."

Wahab replied enthusiastically. "That's a great idea, my dear. It's been a long time since we've been to Rinjani." He looked at Naomi. "I'll talk to your father about it today—and that means," he said as he glanced at his watch. "It's time I went to the office. Come on, girls, off to school." He turned to Noor. "And what about you, son? No classes today. Does the hotel have anything booked for you?"

Naomi's interest was piqued. Noor nodded. "Yes, the hotel has one client for me." Noor rose, kissed his mother, and followed his sisters out of the room.

"And what about you, Farah? When are you and Naomi and Sara going to get the business of Kartini's School off the ground?" Wahab looked at Naomi as he said this, and winked. "Lovely name, by the way."

Farah smiled at Naomi before replying. "Today is a big day. We are going to check out space to rent in Senggigi. There's not much to choose from…but we don't need much."

Wahab kissed his wife and Naomi began clearing the table. She felt excited now, about so many things: about the school, and about family she was getting to know. *Wahab was talking about climbing the volcano!* She couldn't wait to see what her parents would think about Farah's family trip idea.

"Noor, come back here for a moment, will you?" called Wahab. Noor came into the room with a large backpack. "Ah…our trusty mountain guide. Can you please drive Naomi back to her home?"

"Why don't you take her to visit your university after you drop off your sisters," suggested Farah. She turned to Naomi. "You're not in a hurry to get home, are you?"

Noor looked uncomfortable. "I kind of want to get to the hotel early today," he answered. "But I can drop her at home."

"I'll get my things," said Naomi. "I had a great time with you. Thanks so much for inviting me over."

She followed Noor and his sisters to his beat-up car in the drive. Naomi was grateful for the twins' chatter all the way to their school, and felt self-conscious of the silence in the car once they had been dropped off. After a few minutes, Naomi spoke.

"I'm sorry for troubling you—"

"It's no trouble," Noor replied evenly.

"Well, I know you don't want to—" Naomi was trying to say what she meant, but it wasn't coming out right at all.

Noor looked at her briefly. "Why do you think that?"

"Well, I know you weren't too happy to meet us the first time, during the…event in Mataram—"

Noor grimaced. "Oh that…No…you're wrong. I just didn't want to be at that dumb 'parade.'"

Naomi couldn't stop herself from giggling at his surprising reply. Noor looked at her and laughed, too. Naomi felt a wave of relief, and wondered if she and Noor would end up being friends after all.

"Well, I could tell you weren't happy. I thought it might have been something I was wearing—"

"Huh?"

"I was wearing shorts. I know that Muslim women don't do that. I'm sorry. But I know now it's not respectful," Naomi rambled on happily, glad to be getting things out in the open. "I don't—"

"Don't worry about it. All you tourists dress like that—we're used to it."

Suddenly Naomi felt indignant. "I'm not a tourist, you know. I live here. And I'm trying to understand—"

Noor pulled up to Senggigi's only traffic light. He looked across at Naomi. "Well then, you're learning to pray and dress like us. You'll be Indonesian in no time."

Naomi didn't know what to say. She couldn't tell if that was a sarcastic remark or not. She suspected it might be, and was surprised by how unhappy it made her feel at that moment. Little more was said for the rest of the ride.

6

I love Lombok! We are hiking up Mount Rinjani with the Wayuni family. Mom and Farah will head down with Mei-mei now, but the rest of us are going all the way to the summit! Last time I climbed a volcano, I was with Mom in Japan. This time I'm with my Yorkshire dad, and a Muslim family named Wahab, Noor, Jameela, and Fathima. I could never have guessed that this is where I'd be in my life right now, climbing a volcano in Indonesia...

NAOMI LOOKED UP FROM HER JOURNAL. At the other side of the clearing she could see Mei-mei snuggling in her mother's lap. Her mother was speaking to Farah, absently stroking her daughter's hair. Steve and Wahab were seated next to them, listening to Sara talk, content to relax for a while after lunch. Naomi looked down at her last piece of chocolate. She had been saving it for Mei-mei, but decided that she needed it more than her sleepy sister. She popped the piece into her mouth, then put the wrapper and her journal into her backpack and stood up. She was eager to get moving, but it was clear that some of the others in the group were settling down for an after-meal siesta. They deserved a break; it was the second day of climbing, and the two families had already hiked for three hours that morning.

What is it about mountains that always compels me to want to reach for the top as fast as I can? Naomi wondered. She knew she would have to be patient; with two twelve-year-olds in the climbing party, they would have to take things slow. Naomi remembered how she felt when she climbed Japan's Mount Fuji at that age; how it had been the most difficult thing she had ever done, at the time—and the most exhilarating. She smiled, thinking how proud Jameela and Fathima would be when they finally reached the top of Rinjani. Naomi looked around for them; Noor and his sisters had disappeared after they finished eating and were still not back, and now Naomi suddenly felt left out.

"I'm going for a walk," Naomi said to the group, and headed up the path into the trees. Farah had mentioned earlier that there was a special place nearby; it would be the turn-around point for those in the group who weren't summiting. Naomi thought she would go ahead and try to find it on her own.

As she walked through the trees, Naomi thought about the trek ahead of them. She had become a little anxious when Steve had explained that Noor worked part-time as a fishing and hiking guide for the wealthy tourists staying at the resort hotels in Senggigi and Mataram. Naomi had to admit he was good at his job; Noor had been leading them with a self-assurance that demonstrated his abilities and experience. The adults in the group were happy to let him be in charge, and Naomi cold see how proud his parents were, but she also felt put-off by having to listen to his firm instructions about staying on the path, keeping hydrated, and taking rests. Not to mention watching out for snakes. Mount Rinjani was not a simple climb; it was 3,726 metres high, as high as Mount Fuji, and they would be on the volcano for four whole days.

Naomi sauntered down to the edge of a nearby stream, admiring the sound of the babbling water and its purity. She bent down to scoop some in her hand, then remembered that Noor had warned everyone not to drink from the stream. As tempting as it looked, the water had parasites that could cause illness. Reaching behind her, Naomi let it trickle down her back. The coolness, though fleeting, felt good.

Naomi listened. She could hear birds and insects, but could not begin to envision how many different kinds. She took a deep breath, and imagined she could detect singular smells—of flowers and ferns, of decaying plant life, of hidden wildlife, maybe. After several minutes Naomi rose and began following the brook along a faint trail in the foliage. *Maybe this is where Noor and the twins have gone off to,* Naomi thought. She continued to follow the stream's edge, glad to be alone in the hum of the forest. *How many people do I know back home, or in Hong Kong, who have ever done just what I am doing now?* Naomi asked herself. She offered a thank-you to no one in particular, for the chance to be doing this, to be alone in such a place of eternal beauty. The sound of the running water was becoming louder, and Naomi peered through the trees, trying to glimpse the place from where she sensed it was coming. She thought she could make out a sliver of water falling from up high. *A waterfall?* Naomi quickened her pace and within moments she was looking at a ribbon of water rippling down from a rocky ledge, way up above the treetops. Naomi's neck hurt as she looked up, trying to locate the source. There were noises behind her: the cracking of twigs. Naomi turned around and saw Noor and his two sisters emerging from the other side of a rocky outcrop.

"Naomi!" the girls shouted. Jameela and Fathima ran over to her.

"Noor says we shouldn't have picked these," said Jameela. "But they are so pretty don't you think? We got some for your mom and our mom."

"And some for you, Naomi," added Fathima, holding out an orchid and some ferns. Naomi wasn't sure if she should accept the gift under Noor's reproachful eye. She could feel Noor watching her take them. *Well, what am I supposed to do?* she thought, suddenly annoyed at his presence. "Thanks."

The twins looked at each other and giggled. "We're heading back to camp," one of them said. The other laughed some more and followed her sister back along the pathway that Naomi had just taken. Naomi turned to watch their retreating figures. She wasn't sure what else to do. She stared after them, until the two girls were no longer visible, and the sounds of their voices and laughter faded among the trees. *Why did you have to leave me alone with your scary brother?* Naomi thought. She turned to Noor. "I know, they shouldn't have—orchids are lovely, though," said Naomi, as coolly as she could. She looked down at the gift in her hand and then looked around. The sounds of the forest were not enough to fill up the silence between herself and Noor.

"Did you know about that waterfall—and the pool?" asked Naomi, pointing over her shoulder. She knew the answer already, and was annoyed at herself for asking such an obvious question, but it was all she could think of to say. She braced herself for a barb.

To Naomi's surprise, Noor grinned, "Yes. I sometimes bring my trekking clients here to see the falls—if I like them."

Naomi smiled back.

"Did you see the pitchers?" asked Noor.

"Pictures?"

Noor's grin widened. "Pitchers. Pitcher plants. There are flowers next to the falls—they hold water. Come with me. I'll show you."

Naomi followed Noor back to some foliage at the side of a rocky ledge. He reached up and pulled down a large purple flower hanging from vines. "Awesome," Naomi said, peering into the ingenious flower.

"You can drink from this one," Noor said, offering it to Naomi. "Monkeys and orangutans do."

Naomi backed off, not sure if Noor was teasing her. "I thought you said it's not good to drink the water here."

"This is *rain* water," Noor answered. He gently let go of the plant. They watched the flower settle back into place among the vines. "Indonesia has the world's largest flower, too—the *Rafflesia*. When it blooms it smells like rotting meat," added Noor matter-of-factly. Naomi laughed. Noor looked at her and laughed too.

Naomi turned to look at the pool. It was so clear she could see straight through to the bottom, and it looked so inviting that she couldn't resist. "I'm going to stick my feet in, if that's all right with you," she said. Naomi kneeled down to loosen the laces of her boots.

"Good idea," she heard Noor say. Naomi looked up and saw that he was seated on a rock, and was taking off his own boots. "This waterfall is called 'the Hidden Bride.'"

"You mean the falls are her hair, or something?" asked Naomi.

"Yeah. When we don't get much rain, the water doesn't fall. So the bride cannot be rescued from her hiding place in the tree, where the snake put her."

"Are you telling me the local legend? Cool. It sounds like Rapunzel—well, almost," said Naomi.

Noor had placed his boots and socks by the rock, hung his T-shirt on a tree branch, and stepped into the water. He walked in up to his knees, and then dove in, re-emerging at the middle of the pool of water. Noor turned and saw Naomi staring at him in surprise.

"I'm sorry. Did you want some privacy? I was going to bring my sisters here for a swim, like we always do. We come here at least twice a year. At least once a year with my whole family. It's Jameela's favourite place on the whole island." Noor looked off into the trees where his sisters had gone. "Don't know why they took off on me. They don't want to go swimming today, I guess."

"No…no," Naomi said, "you stay here. Go ahead. She was fumbling for words, she knew. She had just removed her socks and was holding them bunched up in her hands. Suddenly Naomi felt out of place; what had been her private space only a few minutes ago had turned into a place where she now felt she was trespassing.

Noor looked intently at Naomi as she spoke. A slow smile spread across his face, and he looked around, at the trees and the ledge from where the water was falling. He took two steps closer to Naomi and held out his hand. "Come in. It's beautiful."

Naomi shook her head. "I can't… don't want to get my clothes wet."

Noor shrugged, and ducked back into the water.

Naomi rolled up her pants and stepped into the pool. "You like it here," she said, before she had a chance to stop herself. It was more of a feeling than a question.

"I love it here," Noor replied.

"Then you must love your job…to be paid to work out here, being a guide."

Noor tilted his head and frowned. "I like being outdoors. I love hiking. But having to listen to foreigners who don't understand…and are…not nice sometimes…That's not fun. Some people think that just because they are rich they don't have to listen. I don't like that. You can't just walk into the Indonesian rainforest, like it's a walk in the park." He looked at Naomi and grimaced. It was a friendly grimace, as though Noor were asking Naomi if she could understand what he was saying. Naomi did not reply. She was thinking how much she wanted to go for a swim, but she couldn't move. She stared at Noor.

"What's the matter?" he asked. "I know you think I'm not as much fun as my sisters—or my parents. I can tell by the way you look at me. Do I scare you?"

Noor's comment caught Naomi off guard. *Are my feelings so obvious?* She shook her head, trying to think of what to say. It was several moments before she could speak. "No…but I think…something's bothering you…yes," she answered, forcing herself to keep looking at Noor.

"You're right. But you haven't lived here all your life and so you don't understand. Indonesia is a complicated place."

"Well, why don't you explain it to me then, Noor?" Naomi replied, hoping that her words did not betray the annoyance she was beginning to feel towards Noor once again.

Noor paused, and Naomi could tell he was thinking of what to say next. "Do you remember, when you slept at our house, my Dad said how religion can cause conflict…"

"Yes."

"Sometimes…if you try to be open-minded, you can get into trouble. It's hard to explain," Noor said. He dropped his arms at his sides.

Naomi nodded, beginning to understand Noor's concerns. It made sense in many ways. "Some people are afraid of what they don't understand. It's like that where I come from too," Naomi said.

"Really? In Canada? Or Hong Kong? Or wherever it is you come from? I'm glad to know that," said Noor. "Even working for the United Nations has gotten Dad into trouble before. Some people think that he shouldn't be working for them. That it's…some kind of bad, Western influence." Noor took a deep breath and continued. "I'm not saying it is. But there are bad influences around here, and some people get confused—"

"What are you talking about?"

"Well, there are a lot of big hotels being built here. Bali is now overcrowded, and some people want Lombok to be another Bali. But the way these hotels are being built is not fair. The developers of these hotels are pushing farmers off their land. The hotels are owned by multinational corporations, by some are also partly owned by friends and relatives of the president, who make sure that the hotels get built."

"I see…"

Noor was standing next to Naomi now, eager to continue. "There has been trouble in the past, the farmers have tried to stop it—the students at the university have tried to help them, too—but we are up against too much. There is a lot of anger, and it is getting stronger."

Naomi nodded.

"And it doesn't help that my mother is going to open up an English school with a foreign business partner."

"But Noor, if that's how you feel about all these foreign … influences, then why do you even bother to learn English yourself? I don't get it."

Noor shook his head and clambered out of the water. He reached for his T-shirt and put it on. When he looked over at Naomi his eyes were blazing, and Naomi found herself nervous once again. "Well, Naomi, I want to work; to have a job. Just like you. With my English I could get a fancy job in Jakarta but I like it here on Lombok and here is where I want to be. For now, my guiding job pays well enough, and I can do what I like. I feel glad that I don't have to spend my days cutting coconuts or fishing for two dollars a day—or selling batik sarongs on the beach. That's just the way it is here, right now, and I am living with it."

Naomi could hear his contempt. *Noor's right. This place is complicated.* "I'm sorry," she mumbled, then headed to a rock and began putting her socks and hiking boots back on. She felt tired all of a sudden, and wanted to get back to her family.

Noor began doing the same. "That's okay," he replied evenly, almost as if the conversation between them hadn't happened. As Naomi tied up her boots, she glanced over at Noor, wondering how he was able to confuse her so much; with a word or a look he could please her, annoy her, make her laugh, or frighten her. She had never met anyone like him before.

• • • • • •

Naomi crawled out of the tent. Wahab, Steve, and Noor were already seated nearby, eating the leftovers of last night's dinner. They looked at her and laughed.

"I thought it was early." Naomi mumbled. She could hear one of the twins stirring in the tent behind her.

"It's never to early to climb mountains. In fact, many people get up in the middle of the night so as to be at the summit for the break of day," replied Wahab. "Isn't that right, Noor?"

"It's going to be a great day to see Lombok from its highest point," said Steve.

Steve had put out a plate of rice and vegetables and a cup of cold tea for Naomi and she sat down to eat hungrily. She was still thinking about the conversation she'd had with Noor the day before, and still full of questions.

"Wahab, what do the foreigners do in Lombok?"

"Well, I think there are about 30 or 40 families living here now. Most of the expatriates are managing the construction of three more resort hotels that are being built here. Some manage the hotels already in operation. Some work for non-government organizations, like your father, doing other things, like roadworks, or irrigation projects."

Naomi nodded. "Do the people like…having foreigners around?"

Naomi could see Noor eyes flicker. Steve and Wahab exchanged amused glances, and Wahab nodded thoughtfully. "Tourism is important. But sometimes it is the way something is done that causes problems—"

"What do you mean?"

"Well, like in so many places, so many countries around the world. Problems occur when people are asked to leave their land. In Indonesia, for example, there have been transmigration programs set up to move groups of people from once place to another, if the government decided it was too difficult to make a living where they were. This—transmigration—has caused a lot of hardship for people, and has even lead to wars between the different ethnic groups. The Madurese have been forced to leave their small island and go to other places, like Java and Kalimantan. I'm sorry to say that they have not always been welcome. Although it works both ways…"

"Are there problems like that on Lombok?" asked Naomi.

"Thankfully no. We seem to get along. We are mostly Muslims; Sasak people, and some Arabs. But there are some Balinese Hindus and a large Chinese community that are Christian or Buddhist as well," Wahab paused and nodded again. "Yes, thanks be to Allah, we all get along."

"What is your family, Wahab?" Naomi asked.

"You mean our ethnic group?" replied Wahab. "We are Sasak. We have lived here on the land for centuries. Lombok has always been a land of rice farmers and, how do you say it now, fishers. But because Bali has become so popular, and because there is no more room to build hotels over there, people want to start building many hotels and golf courses on

Lombok. The government is asking the people to move off of their land to make room—"

"Noor was telling me about that yesterday, and about how some land developers are friends of the president," said Naomi.

Wahab looked at his son for a long time, then continued. "I believe that developing tourism can be helpful to the people here if it is done properly but, yes, cronyism is a problem. As I'm sure you can understand."

"To put it mildly," said Steve.

"And there are plans to build a new international airport," Noor added.

"That would take up a lot of land," Steve said.

"I agree," said Wahab. "If that project were to go through, there would be a lot of displaced people, mostly farmers. There has been talk of such plans for years…I don't know why they cannot just make the Bali airport larger, or build it on reclaimed land over there, just like you did at your airport in Hong Kong."

"I know there will be trouble if that project gets closer to happening," said Noor.

Wahab eyed his son once again, then turned to Steve and Naomi. "Our president does not take kindly to opposition."

Fathima, who had been packing up the tent with her sister, came over. "Can we start climbing now? Jameela and I can't wait any more."

"Good idea," said Steve. "I understand this is your first time summiting Rinjani. You'll have to let me get there first, Fathima, so that I can record the moment for you, with my video camera." Fathima giggled as she scampered back to her sister.

"Let's do it!" Wahab said, punching the air with his fist. "No point sitting around, trying to solve the country's problems all by ourselves."

Naomi decided Wahab was right. She looked up. The jagged peaks of Mount Rinjani's crater loomed above. It was going to be a long day.

7

tujuh

FARAH PUT HER SCISSORS DOWN and rested her arms on the table where she was sitting with Naomi and Sarah. "Only two weeks until we open. I must admit, all this preparation has given me a distraction from my hunger pangs." Farah laughed as she said this, and Naomi laughed with her. It was two weeks into Ramadan, and the Muslim time of fasting. Jameela had been telling Naomi how she was finding the month-long fasting difficult, for her first time.

"I don't know how Fathima and Jameela can do it," said Naomi. "I'm glad that I don't have to—I love my food too much—"

"And so do I, Naomi," replied Farah. "But I believe that this is one way my family can be good Muslims—it is, after all, one of the most important times of our year. I enjoy the practice of cleansing my body, too—it's cheaper than spa therapy from the hotel down the road." She picked up her scissors and continuing to cut out word cards that were piling up in front of her, "And besides, it makes our feasting during *Eid al-Fitr* so much more enjoyable, like a reward that is well deserved."

"I admire your self-control, Farah," said Sara.

Farah looked over at her friend. "And I admire your determination. You must have written a thousand word cards this morning."

Sara sat back, stretched out her arm and rolled her wrist in circles. "Not quite a thousand, although it feels like it. But at this rate, we will be ready to go after *Eid al-Fitr*, with a few days to spare."

"You're right, the celebrations Steve and Wahab have promised us will be for our school opening as much as it will be to mark the end of Ramadan," replied Farah.

There was a knock on the door of their office. A woman peered in, with a young girl and boy at her side. Naomi stood up, *"Selamat pagi."*

The woman smiled in response to Naomi's greeting. "Hello," she said. She turned to Farah and spoke in *bahasa*, as she prompted the two children to enter. Sara and Naomi walked over to shake hands as Farah made the introductions.

"Mrs. Kyew wants to sign up her daughter and nephew," said Farah. She wrote down their names on a list and then spoke briefly in *bahasa* once again before everyone waved goodbye.

"She is excited about our school," said Farah. The three went back to their table and continued to work. After a brief silence, Farah spoke up. "They are a Chinese family."

"Wahab said there are a lot of Chinese in Lombok," said Sara.

"The Chinese community is rather large, for a small place like Lombok," Sara replied. "Mrs. Kyew's family owns a few shops in Mataram—Senggigi too. I don't know her well, but her sons go to the twins' school. I always see her when we mothers are volunteering there."

The doorbell rang again, and Naomi got up to answer it. Noor was standing at the door. He had some flat boxes under each arm.

"It's the whiteboards," said Naomi over her shoulder, and opened the door wide for Noor to enter. "I'll show you where they go." Naomi took some of the boxes from him and placed them on the floor. Noor took a box cutter from his back pocket and began to cut the boxes open. Naomi fetched an electric drill from a small desk in the corner and then pointed to some pencil marks already on the wall at each end of the large room.

"There's an old bulletin board at the hotel, on stands," said Noor, as he drilled holes in the wall and pounded in the plastic plugs. "They were just going to get rid of it and I asked if I could take it off them for free."

Naomi was surprised and pleased by Noor's willingness to help. After the conversation they had had by the waterfall on Rinjani, she suspected he would have not been eager to be involved in getting the English school up and running. "That's so nice of you, Noor!" Naomi said brightly. "It could go over here, to create an alcove for our desk, and we could put a small table next to it, for some one-on-one work with a student, or a special project."

"Good idea," said Farah. "Thank you, Noor. That was very sweet of you."

"We could put a computer there, too," said Sara. "A computer would be very useful—"

"Yes, with all our profits, we could buy a computer," said Farah. There was complete silence in the room for several moments after her remark. She snickered, and then everyone, including Noor, burst into laughter. The laughter grew. Naomi was doubled over, her stomach hurt from the laughter, she could feel tears squeezing out of the corners of her eyes.

Farah put her hand on the table to steady herself, and took a few deep breaths before she could speak once again. "I'm glad to see you are taking this lightly, I know we cannot afford to charge what you say you were earning in Hong Kong and Japan—"

Sara cut in, serious now. "Oh, Farah, Naomi and I never thought about doing this for the money—as you well know. I don't think profit was your motivation, either, Farah."

Farah shook her head. "No, you're right. Of course."

Naomi listened to the women speak, but was becoming more absorbed in her own thoughts. She and her mother had never spoken about why they wanted to open an English school in Lombok. Naomi knew part of it was to avoid boredom, but she also wanted the challenge, and the fact that Farah was their partner had simply made it more fun. But Naomi had always assumed that they would go into business to try to earn a profit. *After all, I'm planning to study business administration, someday.*

"Well, your profits are going to get smaller, whatever you do," said Noor. "The rupiah is falling again."

Sara nodded, her face more serious. "Yes, Wahab says it's going to be a big one this time. It's going to cause a lot of problems for people in Indonesia, he said."

"Let me help you hang this, Noor," said Naomi, trying to change the subject. All of a sudden she didn't want to talk about any more bad news. The school was a good thing. It was going to be good. *Everything is going to be good here, from now on.*

Later that night, after everyone had put Mei-mei to sleep, Naomi and her parents sat in their small back garden. Naomi and Sara told Steve how the English school was taking shape.

"We already have fifteen students. Mostly primary school students, and three high school students. And one adult," Sara said, and Naomi could hear the pride in her mother's voice. "Naomi's going to teach the younger ones. Sara and I are going to teach the high school students together—and I will teach our adult class. I expect we'll have at least double that many students before we even open, though." Sara leaned forward closer to Steve, and she continued to speak more quickly, "We might even open a kind of coffee shop for the hours when the kids are in school. It could be like a drop-in centre, for moms with babies. Farah thinks it's a great idea—"

Steve looked over at his smiling wife, "I'm proud of you both. It makes me happy to know you want to be a part of the community, not just sitting around the hotel pool—"

"No thanks," said Naomi.

Steve smiled at her and nodded, but then his expression changed and he shook his head. "But I have to tell you. You won't make much money—"

"We know that—"

"I don't mean because you don't charge a lot of money for the classes," said Steve, "I mean—because the Indonesian currency is depreciating so quickly—"

"Noor said the same thing today," Naomi said.

"I see. Wahab and I had lunch with him today. It was just before he went to buy your whiteboards," said Steve. He looked into his teacup. "I just hope that the currency can stay afloat a few more weeks, until after Christmas. It would be a pity to lose out when there will be so many foreigners here on holiday at that time. So many people around here depend on the tourism industry."

Naomi and Sara watched Steve in silence. He reached out to hold his wife's hand.

"I'm glad I'm paid in US dollars. But I feel for the local staff. I feel for everyone here. Their currency is in a freefall. Life is going to become a lot more difficult for a lot of people—"

"But isn't that good news for tourists?" Naomi began, trying to understand Steve's concern. "I mean, doesn't that mean lots of people will want to come here because it'll be even cheaper now?"

Steve nodded. "That's true, the fact that Indonesia is a paradise that has become cheaper than ever will attract more tourists—especially ones that don't have a lot of money to spend here—and like to pitch their tents on the beach." He was looking straight at Naomi with a slight smile on his face, and Naomi was beginning to understand what Steve was implying. For all their hard work, Indonesians would now be getting less in return. Like so many things here, Naomi was starting to realize the issue was more complicated that she at first had thought.

·　·　·　·　·　·

Naomi was at the hotel business centre using the Internet. She had a list of things to print out for the school and didn't have much time, but she couldn't resist checking the news. To her dismay she read an item from *The Jakarta Post* about a riot that had broken out in several predominantly Chinese neighbourhoods in that big city. No one was ready to pinpoint a cause, but the devaluation of the country's currency was mentioned. Naomi checked out an Australian newspaper, *The Sydney Morning Herald*, and was even more unhappy to see that the incident in Jakarta had made mention in an Australian paper. Naomi sighed heavily and stared at the computer screen, forgetting about lessons plans and verb lists and word games.

Naomi thought about what Wahab had told her about ethnic rioting in the past. She thought of Mei-mei. Naomi grabbed her bag and left the room, running out past the gate and up the dirt path beside it, to the beach. Naomi threw her bag on the sand and lay down on her back next to it, her breathing was ragged and heavy. *I'm not going to worry!* Naomi forced herself to listen to the sound of the waves. She forced her breathing to slow down, as if in tune to the waves. It took several minutes for Naomi to feel calm once again. She opened her eyes and looked at the palm leaves in the sky above her, and the clear blue cloudless sky beyond. She looked to her right and saw several people laying on the beach, enjoying the day—oblivious to what had just happened in Jakarta, Naomi thought.

It was some time before Naomi returned to the school. She worked steadily through the afternoon alongside her mother and Farah, trying to be as upbeat and excited as she had been feeling all month long. She was glad that both women were preoccupied with the final preparations for the school, and that her mother did not suspect that there was anything

51

troubling her. Naomi wasn't going to tell her, either. The doorbell rang at 5:30, and Farah was soon enrolling two more youngsters for English lessons. At 6:00, Sara, Farah, and Naomi surveyed the newest business establishment in Senggigi: *Kartini's School.* The three looked around their premises with pride. Their shoulders were hunched with fatigue, but their smiles were bright with anticipation. "Well, tomorrow we open," said Sara. "Are we ready?"

"We are ready!" Farah replied. Naomi felt grateful for the self-assurance she heard in her friend's voice.

"That's what I like to hear, Farah," said Sara, laughing. "If anyone had asked me six months ago if I thought I'd be the proprietor of a school in Lombok, Indonesia, I would have—well—laughed!"

The next afternoon, Naomi was standing next to Farah and her mother, listening to her friend and business partner speaking in a language that was becoming increasingly familiar to her ear: "We—Sara, her daughter, Naomi, from Canada, and myself, wish to welcome you to a place you can call your own. A place to learn—about what you can accomplish. Where you can learn English—a language that is spoken by people all over the world." Sara looked at the children sitting by her feet on the carpet and grinned at them. "We hope that you will enjoy this place as the beginning of a new adventure." She looked up at the older students standing against the back wall, and the mothers sitting on the few chairs that were available. "By calling this place 'Kartini's School,' we honour the spirit of that young woman, whom we all know and love," Farah continued. "She understood the importance of reaching out in mind, and in spirit, across countries, across cultures. We hope you will agree that this is one of the best things we can give our children. Thank you for coming here today to mark the opening of Senggigi's only language school—and thank you for your support."

There was polite applause among the forty-four people, most of whom were students or mothers of students. Naomi stood next to Farah and smiled, nervous but excited. After Sara's speech, Naomi served glasses of pineapple juice and mingled with the smaller students, exchanging greetings in English and *bahasa* to the children, who who were clearly as nervous and excited as Naomi was feeling. As the older people began to file out the door, Naomi gathered up the young students whose names were written on a list on the whiteboard at the front of the classroom. It was Tuesday, 4:25 in the afternoon, and a class for children aged five to seven was scheduled to begin shortly. Naomi gulped as she looked at her watch; she was the teacher for that class. It was time to begin.

8

delapan

Today was one of the most awesome days of my life. I don't even have to write down what happened because I know that I'll always remember this day. I went to the Gili Islands with Noor...

"**WHAT ARE YOU GOING TO DO TODAY,** then, on your first—and well-deserved—day off from work?" asked Steve, as he helped buckle Mei-mei into her car seat.

Naomi looked from Steve to Mei-mei, and then to her mother, who was standing on the other side of the Jeep, waiting to hear her daughter's response. "I think I'll head over to the hotel, to catch up on the news. Do some emails. Surf the Net. You know—*stuff*," Naomi answered, hoping that she sounded convincing. Naomi was feeling exhausted from the first week of running Kartini's School, and she just wasn't in the mood to go into Mataram today with Mei-mei and her parents. Normally, Naomi loved jostling her way through the crowded, narrow aisles of Mataram's bustling marketplace, helping her mother and Steve with the shopping and scoping out trinkets for her little sister. But not today. Today, Naomi felt like she needed to be alone.

Naomi could see the look on her mother's face, the one that said 'I don't buy it.' Sara opened her mouth to say something, and Naomi braced herself for the unwanted task of having to explain. But then Sara shrugged, "Yeah, never mind, Naomi, it's a nice day to hang out—you do deserve it."

Naomi walked over to her mother and gave her a big hug. "Thanks, Mom," she said, then crawled into the back seat to give her little sister a squeeze. "Buy some of that sticky rice stuffed into bamboo that I like so much, will you Mei-mei?"

Mei-mei nodded and sang out, "Yes, I like it, too!"

"Will do," said Steve. "Have a good day. Won't be too long."

Naomi waved as the Jeep backed out of the drive then turned down the narrow strip of asphalt in the direction of Mataram. She turned and walked slowly back into the house, now so quiet. Naomi found herself trying to be silent as she gathered some things and put them in her backpack: a bathing suit, her book about Kartini, a hairbrush. She looked at her wallet on the dresser and left it; Steve had an account at the hotel. She headed out the front door and locked it behind her, fully expecting to go to the business centre at the resort, to browse the Internet and maybe spend some time by the pool. A few days earlier, she had come across a section of the *New York Times*. It was called "Portraits in Grief," and in it were stories about every person killed during the Nine Eleven attacks. It had only just been put online, and she was eager to read more.

But as Naomi left her house, the sounds from the beach were calling to her, and Naomi stopped to listen. The waves on the sand, endless and eternal—and always comforting to Naomi—were beckoning. Naomi followed the sound, past the trees, staring straight at the beach and the sea beyond. For a moment Naomi thought of her original plan, and an image of herself formed in her mind: she was seated in front of the computer in the small, rather airless room at the hotel. Then the images of the New York skyline, the twin towers filled with offices, and flames shooting to the sky filled Naomi's mind. People were falling to their deaths; choosing one horrible ending over another...Naomi shuddered. *It's a much better thing, to float away on the sea*, thought Naomi. She strode towards the beach, facing the sea, and all around her the waves, the wind, the sun, the sand— all of them precious elements to her. Naomi kicked off her sandals and dropped her backpack. She lay down on the sand, staring up into the cloudless sky. There were palm fronds breaking into her line of vision. Just green and blue, and the waves…

Naomi opened her eyes. Nothing had changed; there was still just the blue and green, just the sound of waves lapping the beach, the wind in her ears. Naomi looked at her wrist, but saw she was not wearing a watch. *How long have I been sleeping here?* She sat up. No, it wasn't all the same. There was another sound, a faint whirring noise. Naomi turned and saw a small craft emerging from behind the headland at the southern end of the beach. It was a fishing boat, the kind Naomi had seen many times before, except that this one was out on the water at the wrong time of day. It was too late in the morning for good fishing, Naomi knew. She watched the boat come closer, listening absently as the whirring of the boat's small motor grew louder.

Naomi waved. Maybe it was a fisherman she knew, someone she had seen selling fish at the marketplace in Mataram, or Senggigi. She smiled, remembering one particularly cheerful and persuasive fisherman who had eagerly tried out his English trying to sell some of his catch to Naomi and her mother. The boat was getting closer and it gleamed brilliant white in the midday sun. Naomi admired the boat's design; two stripes along the side of the craft were a striking azure blue and a deep crimson. Naomi waved again and then, as soon as she did it, her smile faded. Naomi gulped, and her arms grew slack. Naomi fixed her gaze on the young man seated at the front of the small boat. Naomi could see that the driver was Noor. *Could it be?* There was no doubt about it, Naomi knew. Noor was waving back at Naomi now, and Naomi watched as the boat turned slightly on its new course to the shoreline—and straight towards Naomi. She was still hurting from the fact that he hadn't come to the opening of Kartini's School the week before, nor had he come to dinner afterwards with the rest of his family to celebrate.

Why would Noor be coming in to see me? Naomi wondered if she should just grab her backpack and make a dash to the hotel. *I'll tell him I had some work to do on the Internet. That'll be a good enough excuse to tell him next time I see him, which, hopefully, won't be for a while.* But her feet wouldn't move, and Noor was already so close. The motor chugged noisily now as it drew near. Naomi took a few tentative steps into the waves as Noor cut the engine, not sure what she was supposed to do. As Naomi rested a hand on the side of the boat she looked up at Noor.

"What is it?" Noor said. Naomi thought he sounded annoyed.

Naomi's hand came off the boat, as if she had been burned. "Nothing. I just saw you—"

"Why were you waving at me?"

Naomi took a step back. "I just was waving. I didn't know it was you—"

"Oh."

Noor and Naomi stood looking at each other, as the small craft rocked gently in the waves. Noor began to nod, just as a large wave rolled under the boat, knocking him off balance. Noor's head hit a wooden pole supporting the canopy that protected fishermen from the sun. Noor ducked down reflexively, squinting with pain. He reached up to touch his forehead, and Naomi could see a trickle of blood drip under his hand.

"Noor! Are you okay?" Naomi grabbed the side of the boat, trying to steady it. Noor reached back with one arm to steady himself as he sat down on the bench inside the craft.

Naomi leaned closer into the boat, trying to catch a glimpse of Noor's eyes. "Noor, are you okay—"

Noor glanced up. "I'm okay. Okay," he said dismissively. When he put his hand down Naomi could see a big purple lump had already begun to form where the small cut was.

"Oh, that must hurt—"

Noor's black eyes blazed. "Just a bump," he said. "I thought you were calling me in—"

"NO," Naomi replied—too quickly, and too loudly, it seemed to her, and she regretted it. "No," she said again. "I just saw someone, I saw you. I didn't know it was you. And so, I waved—"

"Well, if you didn't know who it was, why were you waving?"

The sounds of the water around them filled Naomi's ears like white noise. Or maybe it was the sound of blood rushing to her face. Naomi was embarrassed. Good question, she thought. *How can I explain that to a guy like Noor. That I just waved because I didn't care who it was. Because I was just happy to be here, on this beach, on this day. Sad about the world sometimes—and just happy to be alive.* Exasperated, Naomi looked down and shook her head. *He's bleeding from a cut on his head, and he's trying to pick a fight with me. What's his problem, anyway?* Naomi thought, vexed and irritated. When she looked up she saw that Noor was now staring at his hands.

"I'm bleeding."

Noor was looking at Naomi now, bewildered. It was such a surprising image, and his voice all of a sudden sounded so small, that Naomi burst out laughing. In order to cover up what she felt sure Noor would perceive as Western rudeness, Naomi started to try to get into the boat. "Let me check it, Noor," Naomi said as she struggled to hoist herself over the side of the boat. It wasn't as easy as she thought.

Noor grabbed her arm and helped her in, then Naomi and Noor sat together on the bench. Naomi studied the cut and the lump on Noor's forehead. She smiled. "You'll live, Noor. Do you have a first-aid kit on this boat?"

Noor retrieved a small waterproof bag under the bow and passed it to Naomi, who unzipped the top and rummaged through it, looking for a bandage. She pulled out a cotton ball and a small bottle of antiseptic.

"Where are you going?" Naomi asked, as she dabbed at Noor's cut.

Noor sat back on the bench and winced a little. "I—uh—I'm going snorkelling. I was supposed to take some clients from the hotel, but then one of them got an ear infection." And then, all of a sudden, Noor grinned, "I'm off today. What about you?"

"Me? I'm—uh. Well, I was going to go to the hotel. But I kind of, just—"

"Just got stuck here on the beach," Noor finished for her. Naomi nodded and grinned back at him.

"It's easy to get stuck on this beach," Noor said, after a moment. He took the bloody cotton ball and bottle from her. "Come with me—if you want," he said.

Naomi nodded before she had a chance to realize what she had done. "Where will we go?"

Noor started the motor and he shouted above the sputtering noise. Naomi moved over on the bench to give Noor room as he sat down next to the motor. He turned and spoke into Naomi's ear. "We're going to some islands. The snorkelling is great there. There are three islands, very small. Gili Air, Gili Meno, and Gili Trawangan."

Noor and Naomi sat side-by-side as the small craft continued its noisy journey along the water's edge. And while Noor looked in the direction they were going, Naomi looked straight ahead, facing the beach. *It's even more beautiful from this perspective,* she thought to herself. Naomi smiled and inhaled deeply, savouring the salty sea air around them. Slowly Naomi turned to Noor. She was glad that he could not see her looking at him. Noor's posture was relaxed. *I've never seen him so—normal. There was always something on edge about him, whenever I saw him before,* Naomi thought. *But not here…and not in the water on Rinjani…*

And then, just as if he knew she had been studying him, Noor turned around. Naomi sat back against the side of the boat. It was a reflexive action, trying to avoid detection. Naomi's face felt hot, despite the cool sea breeze. She looked over at Noor, and saw that he was smiling.

"Do you know what *gili* means?"

Naomi gulped, "Uh yeah, I assume it means 'island.' Why else would the three islands share the same first word?"

The smile on Noor's lips left momentarily. "You're right. I guess it's obvious. But do you know what *Gili Air* means?"

Naomi shook her head.

"In *bahasa*, *air* means 'water.'"

"Huh? No kidding," said Naomi, grinning. "That's funny. I can use that in one of my English classes. Thanks, Noor."

"You're welcome," replied Noor, looking pleased.

There was silence again. Naomi turned her attention to the shore once more, watching the island of Lombok pass by in front of her. There were some small, local hotels, gardens, rows of palm trees—plantations of some kind, maybe banana or pineapple. From time to time, the main road was visible through the trees, and Naomi could hear a motorcycle whizzing past.

Suddenly Naomi froze. "Noor! I left my bag on the beach—"

"We can go back—"

Naomi thought for a moment. She shook her head, "No, it's all right. It was just a book—and some stuff." She looked at Noor. "Actually Noor," she said, "I don't have any money on me. I didn't need my wallet—"

"Never mind. I don't have any either. The sea is free," Noor said, almost cheerfully. His smile faded, "Oh, but what about a bathing suit?"

"I don't mind swimming in this—this time. No big deal," Naomi replied self-consciously, remembering when they were together on Rinjani. "But if you have a spare T-shirt in your duffel, I'd appreciate it," she added.

"I do," replied Noor. "I have an extra one, and an extra towel, too. And don't worry about lunch. I usually just help myself."

"Oh. Good." *Help myself? What does that mean?* Naomi wondered. She decided she wasn't going to ask, though. It was enough that she was going to spend the day snorkelling in the Gili islands with Noor, who had, for some reason, invited her to come along. Naomi took another deep breath, and let herself relax. *It's easy to get stuck on this beach, Noor said. He knew. He knew what I was feeling. I think he feels the same thing.* She looked over again at Noor, at the wind blowing his hair off his face. *You can't see me now, but I am watching you. I wonder if we are going to be friends after all...*

The boat neared the shoreline. Without warning, Noor jumped out of his boat at the front and into water up to his knees. He began to pull the boat towards the beach.

"I'll get out—"

"No, never mind. No need."

"No, no. I can get out," insisted Naomi. She slid over the side of the boat into the water. She splashed down hard. Her knees buckled and she found herself up to her waist in the sea, and Noor was laughing at her. Naomi looked up at Noor, and the big grin that she was unaccustomed to. Naomi decided she liked what she saw, and grinned back. And then Naomi thought of something else. She pushed both arms deep into the water, and a frothy wave of seawater splashed up at Noor drenching his face and hair and T-shirt. For a moment he looked at Naomi like he couldn't believe what she had done to him, and Naomi wondered whether she should apologize or laugh out loud.

It was Noor who laughed first. It was a wonderful, warm laugh that sounded like it came from the heart.

9

"PERMISI, IBU…" said Naomi to the old woman seated on a stool behind a pile of fruits and vegetables. *"Apa ini?"* she asked, pointing to some red, spiky fruit that Naomi had never seen before.

The old woman chuckled at Naomi, revealing a set of red, betel-stained teeth. *"Rambutan,"* she replied. She peeled the thick skin off one, revealing a soft white inside, and handed it to Naomi. Naomi took a bite, rubbed her tummy, and bought six pieces of the delicious fruit that tasted to Naomi like a combination of lychee, mandarin orange, and coconut. The old woman spoke to her friend at the next table.

"Dari mana?" said the other woman to Naomi.

"Saya dari…Senggigi," Naomi joked, and the two old women chortled at her. *"Saya dari…Kanada,"* Naomi added when the laughter died down. Naomi held up her bag of fruit. *"Terima kasih!"*

"Kembali," replied the old woman, and they waved each other goodbye.

Naomi's arms were laden with an assortment of fruit and vegetables by the time she left the market and headed down the street to Kartini's School. It was Saturday, and she had a morning class of ten children. Today, they would be learning the names of fruit and vegetables, as well as how to buy them, in English. The lesson would be finished off with a huge fruit salad lunch. Naomi was in a happy mood. She knew that three of the students had parents who worked at the market, so the knowledge would be put to good use with any tourists who came by, as they often did. Naomi was humming the tune of an Indonesian song the children had taught her last week as she arrived at the school.

"Naomi, you bring back old memories with that song—" said Farah.

"Good ones I hope," replied Naomi. "By the way, Farah. How do you say *rambutan* in English?"

Farah crawled out from under the computer table, where she had been sorting out a snake-like pile of cables. After a month, the school had become so popular that there were classes every day, and before long it had become apparent that a computer was a necessity that couldn't wait. Steve had bought a second-hand desktop computer and printer from a colleague that was leaving Lombok.

"Uh...rambutan," Farah answered. Her eyes were twinkling as she spoke.

Naomi laughed. "That's what I thought."

Two hours later, Naomi and her students were seated around a table. Naomi looked at all the young faces as they ate the meal they had prepared together. "Delicious!" "Yummy!" "I like it!" "Mango is my favourite fruit!" they exclaimed between bites, happy to be using their new English. Naomi felt proud of her students' confidence and gave herself a mental pat on the back knowing that the children were having so much fun, they probably didn't even realize they were still in class. By the time they filed out the door, giggling and saying their goodbyes, Naomi was buoyed by their energy, exhausted and exhilarated.

"Teaching is hard work," she said to Farah, who was finishing some preparations for her own classes next week.

"But I know you enjoy it, Naomi. Go home and have a rest. You're going to be busy this afternoon helping your mother. Aren't you having company for dinner?" Farah was smiling mischievously.

"You're right. See you tonight."

• • • • • •

"Farah, Sara...Wahab, I'd like you to meet Mike. He's a bush pilot from Australia, working on a project over in Kalimantan province, on Borneo," said Steve, standing next to a tall man in the living room. Wahab rose to shake hands with Mike, who then circled to room to shake hands with Farah and Sara. "And this is Naomi, my daughter," added Steve, when Naomi entered the room with a tray of drinks.

"Lovely!" said Mike, as he took a drink and smiled at Naomi. "The drink, that is," he added. The others in the room laughed. "And you too, darling...I sure need one of these. I've just been on a hell of a ride."

Naomi could feel herself blushing. She could tell that Mike was a different kind of character, just by his wrinkled khaki trousers and bright batik shirt. His hair was wavy and unkempt as well, and on his deeply tanned face he sported week-old stubble. His friendly and open demeanour made Naomi warm up to him at once. He was such a contrast to Steve, though. Naomi wondered what Farah and Wahab and her mother thought of this colourful Australian stranger Steve had brought home.

"Mike's just come in for a quick break. It's unbelievable what he's been doing over there," said Steve, shaking his head. "He's supposed to be ferrying in geologists…and ends up evacuating 50 Madurese—"

"Well, more than 120 actually," said Mike between sips of his drink. "I went back a second time—" Mike peered into his glass. "I'm afraid I left many behind."

"The problem there has boiled over once again," said Wahab gravely. He looked over at Farah and at Mike again.

Naomi could see how bright Farah's eyes were, but this time she was not happy. "Such a tragedy," Farah said, blinking hard.

What are they talking about? Naomi wondered. *Why is there so much about this place I don't know?* "What's the problem in Kalimantan?" she asked.

"Well, Naomi, you remember what I said about transmigration? There are reports of fighting between different ethnic groups there," Wahab began. "There are the indigenous Dayak people, and a large group of people who immigrated to the larger island of Borneo from their own island of Madura. The Madurese are outnumbered…A good example of bad race relations—"

"They're being slaughtered!" Mike cried out. The room became silent, but for the ice tinkling in Mike's shaking glass. He looked at the people around him and shook his head. "I've seen it," he whispered.

Naomi couldn't breathe. She stared at the man who only a few minutes earlier had seemed wonderfully eccentric—and was now almost trembling next to her.

"Mike, can I get you something stronger?" asked Sara.

"Naw, I'll be right."

"Listen, it's getting late," said Steve. "Let's start dinner—"

"But Noor's not here yet," said Sara.

"I don't know what's keeping him," replied Farah, "but I think we should get started."

Everyone rose and headed to the dining table, Wahab gave Mike a reassuring pat on the shoulder as they sat down at the table.

"Naomi, would you sit next to your father—and we'll keep the seat next to you for Noor, when he gets here," said Sara. Naomi did as she was told, still taken aback by what had just played out between Wahab and Mike in the living room.

"I'd like to say a toast…and give thanks," said Wahab, after everyone was seated. He looked around the table and smiled. "I'd like to say how pleased my wife and I are to be here with our friends. We thank you for your friendship…and for your courage," he added, raising his glass of juice to Mike. Wahab looked over at his wife, who smiled back at him lovingly. Wahab turned to Sara. "You have given my wife a chance to become a businesswoman. This is something that I know she has always wanted to be." He was chuckling, and Farah's sweet laughter filled the small room. "And so, my wife and I toast to you—to us all—for a long friendship."

"To long friendships, I reckon," added Mike, as he raised his glass.

"So Farah, is what Wahab saying true?" asked Steve as plates of food were being passed around. "Is Kartini's School in the black yet?" He smiled over at Sara and continued, "I don't know. It seems that Sara doesn't want to divulge too much about the books—"

"Steve!" Sara shot back. "That's not true!"

Steve chuckled, "I know she's enjoying it, though—"

"I am, too," said Naomi. "We got four new students this week."

"We've got classes five days a week now."

"And an evening adult class on Wednesdays—with five students," said Farah proudly.

"I know," laughed Steve, "that's the day I'm on dinner duty—"

"What do you mean, Dad?" retorted Naomi, "I help you." Everyone laughed. The banter around the dinner table had become jolly.

"I love that class," said Sara. "One of my students is a woman who has been working as a maid at the resort since it opened."

"Ibu Soejarno. Yes. I've known her for a long time. She told me that she used her English for the first time. She was so pleased," said Farah. She looked over at Naomi and her eyes sparkled, "And you know what else? We have received several kind words from mothers about how their children are enjoying their classes with Naomi. You should be very proud of yourself. You are obviously a good—"

The doorbell rang and Noor was in the dining room before anyone had a chance to get up and open the door.

"Noor why are you so late? It's almost ten—"

Naomi's heart began to pound. He was standing in the doorway, panting, speaking rapidly in *bahasa* to his mother and father. Then Farah gasped and put her hand to her mouth. Wahab was speaking loudly to Noor. Naomi was confused. *Is Wahab angry?* And then Naomi's stomach lurched. Mei-mei had gone there to spend the night with Jameela and Fathima. *Something bad has happened over at Noor's place!*

"Farah?" said Sara, grabbing her friend's arm.

Wahab turned to Sara. "Don't worry, any of you. Mei-mei and our girls are fine. There is nothing wrong at our home. Noor has just told me some terrible news…some monstrous news. There has been some sort of attack in Bali. Bomb blasts at a nightclub. Many are dead."

"My God!" whispered Sara. Farah slipped her arm around Sara's.

"I heard about it at the hotel," said Noor.

Steve stood up. "I've lost my appetite. I'm going to put the television on."

Everyone headed back into the living room and were staring in shock and disbelief at what they were seeing on television. It was chaos. A reporter was explaining that a popular nightclub in Kuta, one of the most touristed sections of Bali, had been destroyed by two large explosions. Naomi could see medics moving injured people on stretchers. "The building has been obliterated. Neighbouring buildings have also been destroyed. Blocks are burning. Scores are dead. Many injured, trapped under debris. It was crowded, of course. It is Saturday night…"

Naomi looked around the room, remembering the morning when she and Steve and her mother had been sitting in a hotel room in Jakarta watching the unfolding horrors of Nine Eleven on television. The feelings flooded back into Naomi, as if it were happening all over again. It was.

"And now, this," whispered Farah.

No one responded to Farah's sad lament. Everyone continued to stare dumbfounded at the television, as the announcer continued to explain the things that no one wanted to believe.

"…no country is immune, it seems…"

"What is happening to my country? My beloved country," Wahab cried out. Naomi's heart pounded inside her chest. Tears filled her eyes as she stared at Wahab, who put his head in his hands and wept.

10

"I'M GOING," SAID NOOR.

Naomi looked up. She and Noor had been sitting on the beach, sipping water from the coconuts that Noor had brought. Naomi could see Noor's determination.

Go where? Naomi was tempted to reply. But she knew what he was going to say. She knew what he was thinking. Naomi had been up all night, thinking the same thing. "You're going to Bali," she said quietly. It wasn't a question.

"Yes. I am. I want to—*do something!*"

"What do you think you can do?"

"I don't know." Naomi thought she detected a hint of desperation in Noor's voice. "But there's got to be something I can do."

Naomi looked at the coconut in her hands, and was silent. Part of her felt nervous about Noor and his plan; part of her wanted to go with him. She wanted to do something, too. She knew they might just end up getting in the way of the people that were already there, already helping save the injured, along with those that were clearing up the site of the terrorist explosion. She and Noor and their parents, and Mike, had sat up until well past midnight watching the television. She remembered feeling so helpless, and she still did. When she had finally gone to sleep, she awoke to learn that the tragedy in Bali was not a dream but was still happening; people were still being found in the rubble of the buildings that had been destroyed by the bomb blasts.

Naomi hated this helpless feeling. *There's got to be something we can do!* An idea flashed into Naomi's mind. She turned to Noor. "We can give blood. I know they'll be needing blood, if there are so many injured—"

"Good idea!" Noor said. "We'll make our way to Mataram, find some way to get to Lembar, take the hovercraft from there—" Noor then stopped, looking intently at Naomi. "You want to go with me?"

"If you're going to Bali, to try and help, then I'm going with you," Naomi replied. "I want to help too, you know. I feel the same way you do about this—about what happened." It was hard to even put words to; the unspeakable act, the horror. Naomi still caught herself wondering if it was all a nightmare, and wishing that it were.

"Thank you, Naomi," he said. There was a momentary silence as the two sat looking at each other; Noor ended it with a self-conscious, nervous chuckle. "So…who's going to tell our parents what we're doing?"

"We don't have to tell them the whole truth. We can just say we're going snorkelling at Gili Trawangan for the day—or something."

"That will do for now—just as long as our little sisters don't beg to come along." He rose and helped Naomi get up off the sand. "I'll meet you at the bus stop in front of the hotel in half an hour."

Naomi turned and ran through the palm trees to her home. Before half an hour had gone by, Naomi and Noor were on their way to Mataram, where they would then have to find another mode of transport to the pier at Lembar, where the hovercrafts to and from Bali docked. Naomi and Noor were sitting in the back of a half-ton truck, among sacks of coconuts and several other people who had flagged down the vehicle. The driver, a friend of Noor's, had stopped at the bus stop where they had been waiting and had offered them a lift. It was the most popular mode of transport on the island; a common way for neighbours to help each other out.

Naomi looked out over the green rice fields and palms of Lombok as they headed south. The wind was blowing Naomi's hair everywhere. It was not easy to talk; the wind would simply carry their words away into the warm air. But Naomi didn't want to talk. She was feeling nervous about going to Bali. She was terrified of what she would see. She also felt guilty about going with Noor, and not telling her mother or Steve the truth. She had left a note on the kitchen table, saying that she was going to Gili Trawangan with Noor again, just like she and Noor had agreed, but now, as she thought about her actions, Naomi felt ashamed. It had been a long time since she had lied to her mother. Naomi sighed. Her mother and

Steve would have never allowed her to go over to Bali. Not alone with Noor—and definitely not now, not after this unspeakable tragedy.

Naomi looked over at Noor, who was trying to have a conversation with one of the men sitting in the back of the truck. Naomi watched them for a moment, the two of them sitting side-by-side and talking into each other's ears, trying to make themselves heard. Naomi watched Noor speak; then the man looked up at Naomi and their eyes met. Embarrassed, Naomi looked away, wondering what he was thinking and if he was thinking about her, a Western girl going off someplace alone with a Indonesian boy—a Muslim boy.

Naomi turned her attention to their destination. Bali. She tried to imagine the scene that would meet them on arrival. Already the news event had been given a name by the media: *The Bali Bombing*. It seemed odd, Naomi thought; to give such a horrible, destructive, deliberate act a name like that made it seem somehow more acceptable, as if it were a story that had been written, and that that was simply the title—just like *The War in Iraq*, or *The Attack on the World Trade Center*. Naomi remembered seeing these headlines on television. It was like they had become TV programs, a horrible soap opera; it had its cast of characters, Osama bin Laden, al-Qaeda; it had its main setting; Ground Zero in New York City, where the World Trade Center had once stood. And now, Naomi realized that she was heading to the place that featured in this latest chapter in the unfolding story of worldwide terror.

Naomi pictured the images she had seen on the television and on the Internet: the carnage in the crowded tourist area of Bali; several blocks of bars, shops, and restaurants near Kuta Beach. It was a popular place; the surf was world-renowned. It was where Australian students liked to celebrate after graduation and where families from all over the world loved to spend their holidays. Kuta was popular with people living in Hong Kong, too, Naomi knew—Jovita had spoken of Bali before. In fact, the more Naomi thought about it, the more Naomi remembered that many people she'd met in Hong Kong had spoken of this lovely place, known for the beauty of its countryside and for the warmth, charm and beauty of its culture. Bali was different from much of the rest of Indonesia; a tiny Hindu island within a predominantly Muslim archipelago.

Naomi tried to remember what she had learned about how the Hindu influence travelled to Bali from India, and stuck, but she couldn't. More images from the Internet flashed into her mind—photos that she had seen on the computer early that morning at the hotel business centre—a middle-aged man, his face bloodied, being led away from the destruction behind him. The man looked afraid but uncomprehending at the same time, it had seemed to Naomi; as if the scene around him was just too much to take in.

The truck hit a bump in the road, and the image flew from Naomi's mind. Naomi looked at Noor, and saw that he was already looking at her; the shy smile on his face told her that he knew his secret gaze had been discovered. Naomi returned the smile, just as another wave of fear washed over her. *Are we doing the right thing?* Suddenly Naomi realized that she had made an impulsive decision, and was in the process of regretting it— not only lying to Steve and her mother, but also going to a place of danger and chaos. *Maybe whoever did this will strike again! Maybe these terrorists— if that's what this really is—are not finished. Why did I lie?*

Naomi felt a hand on her shoulder. Noor had crawled over and was crouched beside her, just as the truck hit another large bump in the road. The force knocked Noor over and he fell hard next to Naomi. Noor reached across to steady himself, scrambling to gain his balance.

"Are you okay, Naomi?"

"Yes, I'm fine. I'm fine."

He mumbled an apology, and Naomi felt sure she saw his face grow red from embarrassment. In that instant, it was as if Naomi's anxieties lifted. She looked at the young man and smiled, almost giggled with joy, grateful just to be with him on her way into a place of danger, but also because she liked Noor; she liked him more with each day they spent together; for all his confusing behaviour with her, and everything Naomi thought she knew, or didn't know, about him, she knew he was a caring person—who cared about her.

"Are you having second thoughts?" Noor asked.

"I was," Naomi replied. "But not now." Naomi paused momentarily, then corrected herself, "I mean, I really don't like having to lie to my parents. But as for going to Bali—to try to help—no, I don't have regrets. I'm not afraid." Naomi wasn't sure if she believed her own words.

Noor smiled. It was another genuine, wide-open smile. He slipped his arm through Naomi's and held her hand tightly. "Thank you for coming with me, Naomi. Thank you for thinking of how we can help. Giving blood is a good idea." He stopped short and frowned. "Have you ever been to Bali?"

"No."

"I'll take care of you. Don't worry."

Naomi let out a deep breath, and let her body relax. Her head rested on Noor's shoulder. It happened without her letting it, and she jerked her head back upright when she realized what had happened. The driver stopped short for a dog in the road, and Naomi and Noor were thrown together once again. Everyone in the back of the truck were scrambling, grabbing onto the side of the truck, looking around at each other and grinning sheepishly. And then, a few moments later, the truck was pulling off the main road. They had arrived at the bus terminal by the pier.

The bus terminal was a potholed pavement sectioned off by concrete platforms, each fronted by a faded sign with numbers on it. There was one brightly coloured bus sitting idle, from a resort hotel Naomi knew was located on the southern coast of Lombok, and two empty taxis. Naomi saw the hovercraft about 100 metres away and, next to it, a blue and white ship that looked like it needed some repair work. Naomi noticed that there were a few tourists heading onto the hovercraft, while the other vessel looked deserted. There was a palette of boxes containing canned goods and other household items on the ground in front of it, waiting to be picked up and taken to local shops. Naomi realized that the price of the hovercraft ticket was going to be much more than the cost of taking the boat. *Noor probably doesn't have much money*, she thought.

"Noor, we can take the boat—"

"No, it's not going for a couple of hours. And it takes about six hours, anyway. I want to get there as fast as we can," Noor replied, pointing to the hovercraft and heading in its direction.

Naomi fell in behind Noor, wondering if she should offer to help pay for his fare, but decided against it. Noor wouldn't like that, she knew. They bought tickets at the small prefabricated booth on the pier then entered the hovercraft along with a busload of German tourists who had come from one of the resorts. Naomi knew more than a few words of German, but she did not need to be German to understand what they were talking about. They were heading to Bali in order to leave Indonesia, cutting short their holidays in the wake of the bombing at Kuta. They were afraid. Some were angered. Naomi looked around her, at the other passengers in the half-filled hovercraft and realized that probably most of them were doing the same thing, trying to get as far away from Bali and Lombok as they could. Again, Naomi found herself wondering if she was doing the right thing. She turned to Noor. He was gazing out the window as the hovercraft began to leave the pier.

"How long is this hovercraft ride, anyway? I'm not even sure." Naomi asked, flustered.

"It's about two hours."

"That long? I didn't realize it was that far."

"It's a pretty wide strait between Bali and Lombok," replied Noor. "On a windy day, it can get pretty choppy, too. It's better to take this than the ferry, in case you're the kind that gets seasick."

"I am, actually," said Naomi. Noor reached forward and pulled out a motion sickness bag from the seat pocket in front of him. He handed it to Naomi, and they both laughed.

By the time Noor and Naomi got off the hovercraft at the pier in Sanur, Bali, Naomi was feeling wobbly. She had tried to sleep off a growing nausea; the wind was brisk and, just as Noor had warned, the seas had become rough for an hour as they were midway between the two islands. It took Naomi several minutes to realize that Noor was holding her arm at the elbow to steady her as they walked down the gangplank into the chaos that was Bali.

11

sebelas

NAOMI'S GROWING NAUSEA FADED when she stepped off the hovercraft in Bali. Although she was relieved to be on firm ground again, what she saw around her made the nausea dissipate under a wave of growing panic. Naomi could see the drab olive colour of military personnel and armoured vehicles everywhere she looked. It was unexpected; so many people, both in Indonesia and in other places she'd been, had told her of the beauty of Bali. Naomi remembered Jovita saying it was one of her most favourite places. It hardly seemed possible now.

Naomi's eyes came to rest on a female soldier stationed at the bottom of the gangplank, who was checking people's passports as they came off the hovercraft. Naomi and Noor descended, and Naomi nervousness turned to fright when the policewoman looked intently at her, and then at Noor. The officer spoke abruptly to Noor as they passed, and Noor replied in a calm manner. The woman's eyes widened a little, and she spoke again to Noor before waving them through and turning her attention to other passengers.

Noor took hold of Naomi's hand, leading her away from the pier and towards the street where buses and cars and trucks were jammed among the military vehicles in a slow-moving throng. "She thinks we should have stayed in Lombok, but suggested we try going to the hospital here in Sanur, just down the road," Noor offered. "That's where I was planning to go, anyway."

Noor and Naomi jogged alongside the traffic-filled streets. The sun was hot and already Naomi was thinking of water, grateful that Noor had bought a bottle on the hovercraft. "No point taking the bus, it's faster to walk—" Noor began. Naomi was disappointed in herself, and realized that the policewoman was right; they were only adding to the confusion.

Naomi chided herself for not realizing the effect that the bombing would have on traffic in the area. For a moment Naomi was ready to say to Noor that they should forget about this crazy plan and return to Lombok, but the determination on Noor's face told her what his response would be.

A taxi honked just behind them, and both turned to see a young man, the driver, waving them over to his car. Noor walked over and stuck his head in the window, talking for a moment while continuing to walk alongside the slow-moving vehicle. He waved Naomi over. "He thought you were heading to the airport. He was going to give you a lift with these people," Noor explained.

Naomi smiled grimly and shook her head in response to the taxi driver and the three tourists in the back seat. "Does everyone here think all the foreigners are leaving Indonesia now, likes rats from a sinking ship?" Naomi asked, as she and Noor cut through the cars to the other side of the street.

Noor nodded. "Who can blame them? I'll bet a lot of people are going to lose their jobs. With all the tourists clearing out, a lot of business will be lost. The hotels are going to be empty—"

"I thought you didn't care much for tourists," Naomi replied. She meant for it to be a lighthearted retort, but it didn't come out that way. It sounded reproachful.

Noor kept looking straight ahead as they walked. "This place cannot survive without tourists." After a pause, Noor added, just as reproachfully, "I don't hate my job, you know. I don't hate foreigners, I told you that before. It's just that…how would you like being a guest in your own home?"

Naomi was taken aback by Noor's remark, but, more than anything else, she didn't want to get into an argument with him now. Not when she needed him to get home at the end of the day. "I'm sorry," she said, trying to understand Noor's anger. She began to think about what he meant by being a guest in your own home.

They continued walking down the sidewalk past columns of stopped vehicles. A policeman on a motorbike drove by on the sidewalk in an effort to bypass the traffic-choked street. The officer peered at Naomi from behind dark glasses and continued forward, looking in the windows of every vehicle. *I wonder what he's looking for?* Naomi thought. *Is he looking for terrorists?* A chill went down Naomi's back in spite of the heat. Noor picked up his pace and started jogging. Naomi tried her best to keep up and in five minutes they were standing in front of the hospital, a large butter-coloured building. There were crowds of people milling in front of it. Soldiers were stationed at the entrances. Naomi realized that she and Noor would not be allowed near the building if they weren't injured victims or, at least, family of the injured.

Naomi and Noor stood for several minutes watching the crowd, not sure of what to do. No one seemed to see them, or care that they were there. Naomi noticed that the crowd in front of the hospital was a mix of foreign tourists—a lot of them sun-burned—and Indonesian people. Many in the crowd were crying inconsolably, some were clearly in shock, huddled mutely in groups, holding hands, physically and emotionally exhausted. A group of women, Australians, Naomi thought, were shaking and holding onto one another for support, their brightly coloured evening dresses torn and blackened, and splattered with blood. Naomi imagined them partying the night before, oblivious of the monstrosity that was about to confront them all. She watched in silence as these young women listened to a man speak, and from the conversation Naomi guessed he was from their consulate. The man was writing on a pad. "What are their names?" Naomi heard him say. One woman began nervously naming her friends, and another began to wail. Her knees appeared to buckle, and she reached for the woman standing next to her, who grabbed her and held her up.

Naomi choked back a sob. Noor took Naomi's hand and led her through the crowd. He walked up to a police officer and began to speak, and the officer pointed off to the side. Naomi let Noor lead her through the crowd to a tent that had been set up at the side of the hospital. Two more soldiers were standing at the entrance, and Naomi watched them nodding as Noor spoke to them, and then look over at her and nod again. Naomi's breath caught when Noor led her into the tent, she could see it was a makeshift blood donation centre. Five people were seated in lounge chairs: two nurses were attending to the blood donors. Naomi turned to look at a table nearby. It was covered with a pristine white tablecloth, and laden with plates of sandwiches and cookies. A man in surfing gear was helping himself to a glass of juice from a large plastic dispenser. Naomi saw the bandage on his arm; he had already donated his blood. She noticed the napkins on the table had the name of a well-known resort hotel on it. She looked at the tablecloth again, white and clean, and she thought again of the women she had seen, and their blood-spattered party dresses.

It seemed quiet inside the tent, Naomi realized, eerily quiet, compared to the noise and confusion and emotion among the crowd outside. "Are you here to donate?" asked one of the nurses, as she helped a donor, an Indonesian man, to his feet. She turned to the man, and urged him to help himself to the refreshments.

"Yes," replied Noor. He lay down on the lounge chair and said, with an awkward smile, "I've never done this before."

The nurse responded warmly, but wearily. "Thank you for coming. There are a lot of wounded." The nurse was wiping Noor's arm with a cotton swab.

"Do you know how many?" Naomi asked, seating herself gingerly at the foot of the lounge chair Noor was laying on.

"I'm not sure. More than 100 people, maybe. I don't know how many of those are dead, how many are wounded. There will be more to come, I imagine," the nurse replied, shaking her head. For a moment it looked to Naomi as if the nurse was about to cry.

No one spoke as the nurse pressed the needle into Noor's arm. He watched, Naomi noticed, and did not flinch. Naomi hated getting needles. She had never donated blood before, either.

"What is your blood type?" asked the nurse when she began to prepare Naomi's arm a few minutes later, when another donor had vacated the chair next to Noor.

"B negative, I think."

The nurse's eyes shot up, and Naomi thought she could detect a slight smile. "Your blood is rare. You could sell it," the nurse said, then grinned. "I'm sorry we are not buying it today."

"I'll take the food," Naomi replied, forcing herself to smile back.

"You're welcome to it," the nurse said, then explained how the procedure would work. She gave Naomi's hand a reassuring squeeze before heading to another corner of the tent.

Naomi and Noor lay quietly, looking around at the strange and surreal surroundings, their blood dripping bright red into the plastic bags hanging next to them. After several more minutes, Noor's bag of blood was full and a nurse came over to remove the tube from his arm. He was making his way to the table of food when shouts came from outside the tent.

"No room there! Bring 'em this way!" Naomi heard. Seconds later, paramedics burst into the tent, carrying three people on stretchers. The nurses ran to the two empty lounge chairs and adjusted their seat backs, so that they lay flat like beds.

"Over here!" shouted the nurse who had spoken with Naomi earlier. She turned to Naomi and whispered, "Don't worry. Just another five minutes and you'll be out of here." The tent was filling up with wounded and those carrying them in. She could see bloodstains on the white sheets that covered them, and blackened faces. Naomi began to notice a new smell, and with increasing alarm she realized it had to be the smell of charred, burned flesh.

"If you don't need to be here, please leave the area!" someone shouted. "Thank you donors, please help yourself to the food, take it outside!" Naomi began to panic. As long as the needle was in her arm, she could not leave. Her eyes searched the crowded tent for Noor. She saw him heading towards her and felt relief wash over her. And then, just as quickly, Naomi watched someone stop Noor, and he then was being shown the exit. Naomi could see Noor beginning to argue and pointing in her direction, but the man was firm and he grabbed Noor on the arm and began leading him outside the tent.

Their eyes met. "I'll wait for you," Naomi thought she heard Noor say over the commotion. She nodded, hoping that the fear she was feeling could not be read on her face. Naomi sat, terrified, as a man, blackened and bloodied, was being lowered onto the chair next to her. She watched as the medics worked; removing what they could of his charred clothing and assessing his injuries. Naomi wished she could understand what the medics were saying.

"More?" asked the nurse to the medics. There was anxiety in her voice. Another burned body was being brought into the tent. This time there was an Australian helping to bring him in.

"We're finding 'em under things, now. It's carnage!" Naomi heard the blond man say. She craned her neck to see. It was a woman this time, being laid behind the food table, the only space left in the tent. The people who had been working on the man next to Naomi had turned their attention to the new patient.

"I've got this one!" the nurse cried out. She set up an I.V. drip next to the man, then glanced at Naomi's bag of blood, that was by now almost full. She looked at Naomi, almost apologetically. "Only a few minutes more." She looked at the man, then at her, and Naomi could tell she was thinking of something to say. The nurse rested her hand on Naomi's arm and leaned close to her ear. "Don't look," she whispered. Then she was gone.

Naomi realized that she was starting to hyperventilate, and she tried to slow down her breathing. *Don't need to be afraid,* she told herself. Slowly she turned to look at the face of the injured man lying next to her. She thought that he might be middle-aged. But the rest of him did not look human. His body was charred. It didn't look real. Blood and bodily fluids, blackened clothing, flecks of something coloured a bright blue—*what was it—could it be metal? wood? sticking out of the man's burned body?*

God.

Naomi froze. It was barely a whisper, but Naomi was there, and she had heard it. The man spoke. Naomi looked around the tent, hoping that someone was coming to her, and to the man next to her. But everywhere in the tent, everyone seemed to be busy with new cases of injured. "Somebody," she croaked. Her breath was strangled. "Somebody."

Why.

Naomi turned to the man again. She could hear his voice through the ragged sounds of his laboured breathing. She could see his chest rising and falling slowly, faintly. It didn't seem possible in a body so damaged.

Naomi swallowed hard and looked around the tent again. No one was coming to help this man. They were all busy; they didn't notice what was going on in this corner of the tent. The commotion, the attention was elsewhere. Naomi, panic stricken, turned back to the man. She could see his lips moving. Naomi sat up slowly in her chair, careful not to upset the stand on which the bag of her blood was hanging. She stifled a gasp when she saw more clearly the extent of the man's injuries. Although Naomi had never seen death before, she knew that this man was not going to live much longer. Slowly, Naomi leaned a little closer to him. She looked around the tent one last time, hoping a nurse would be on her way to save him. Naomi swallowed hard. "Don't worry… Please… Don't worry," she whispered. She reached over to touch a finger on the man's hand. One finger that seemed unburned; flesh beneath a layer of dirt and soot. The man spoke, and Naomi focused all her attention on listening, trying to understand what he was saying.

I didn't do anything.

Was that what the man said? It was not clear; Naomi thought she might have imagined it. His eyes fluttered. Naomi looked down at her hand, and the man's hand beneath it. She looked at his face. His breathing was shallow, almost as if it weren't even there. Naomi gasped. "Hold on!" she whispered hoarsely, to this man she did not know, but in that instant knew it was important she was there with him. Even so, panic jolted Naomi. She didn't want this man to die. She couldn't believe he was dying; didn't want to believe it. *"Hold on!"*

Five minutes later, one of the medics was leading a distraught Naomi out of the tent. Noor was waiting at the entrance. Naomi took several steps forward and fell into his arms. "Take me home," she sobbed. Noor held her tight, and together they staggered through the crowd, Naomi not noticing how the crowd moved out of their way, and all the people looking at her, seeing that she herself was uninjured, and wondering who it was she had lost.

Naomi couldn't talk on the hovercraft ride back to Lombok. It would be dark by the time she arrived home, and she would have to tell the truth about what she and Noor had done that day. Naomi wasn't sure if she would have the strength to deal with her parents when the time came, but, at least for now—at this moment—there was peace again. For as long as she sat in her chair in the hovercraft, there was peace. She held Noor's hand in silence, and said a prayer for the man who had died, wondering who he was and who would be crying for him that night.

12

dua belas

I'll never forget what happened in Bali. And the man next to me. He died—it's hard to even write that down. He said: I didn't do anything. I wonder what he meant. Did he mean that he didn't do anything to deserve being killed? Did he mean something else? What does a dying person think? What does someone do when they know they are going to die? How many people can know that?

NAOMI STOPPED AND STARED at the words on her page for a long time before continuing:

My friend Chen would have known, when he jumped in the water to save those drowning boys. I think he knew he could drown, but he went in anyway. I wonder what makes someone do that?

*Maybe that man thought he hadn't made a difference, in his life…and now he knew he had run out of chances…*Naomi thought, as she continued to write in her journal. It was Monday morning, and she hadn't spoken much to either of her parents on her return from Bali. She hadn't told them yet what she and Noor had done the day before. Naomi was dreading it. She wanted to tell her parents the truth, not just because the truth was important, but because she felt she needed someone to talk to about it, about what she had seen, and about how afraid she had felt. Naomi knew that there would be a major confrontation. She knew her mother would be angry beyond words, and Naomi wanted to put it off as long as she could. She stared at the pages of new writing, trying to sort out the jumble of feelings and thoughts. Writing things down helps, thought Naomi, *but it's not enough now.*

Naomi looked around her room, at the curtain fluttering in the breeze. She put her journal down on the floor next to her bed and lay down, staring at the ceiling fan. She could hear Mei-mei and her parents in the kitchen. Steve was getting ready for work. *Steve's leaving soon and I should come out to say goodbye—but I don't want to get up off this bed.* Then the phone rang and Naomi stiffened.

"Oh, hello Farah!" Naomi heard Sara say in her cheerful morning voice.

Naomi held her breath.

"What?…No, she didn't…Yes, it's unbelievable…She never said a word."

Naomi let her breath go in a long, resigned sigh. There was a pause before Naomi heard her mother speak again. "Farah, can I get back to you, please? I'm going to talk to Naomi right now."

Naomi heard her mother hang up the phone. She lay inert on her bed, straining to hear the muffled conversation her mother was now having with Steve in the kitchen. "I want to talk to her," Naomi heard, and then her mother's footsteps. Naomi sat up on the edge of her bed and looked at the open doorway, steeling herself for the inevitable.

"Naomi. Where were you and Noor yesterday?" Sara's voice was controlled and tight in her throat, but her blazing eyes betrayed her rage. Naomi was shaken, not sure if she had ever seen her mother so angry.

Naomi looked straight ahead, trying to gain composure. "I know I should have said something—"

"You should have said something?" Sara reiterated. Her eyes were wide, and her face was flushed. She stood in the doorway with her hands on her hips.

Naomi looked down at her own hands resting in her lap. "I'm sorry," she whispered. She was surprised to see a large tear splash on her fingers. *I held his hand.*

"God, Naomi. What's wrong with you?…Naomi…How could you?"

"I'm sorry!" Naomi cried out, looking up at her mother. *"I'M SORRY!"* she screamed. Naomi wrapped her arms around herself and leaned forward. She bowed her head as far as she could, with her hands clasped over it, trying to cover her ears with her arms to shut out the world. *Where can I curl up and hide?* She rocked at the edge of the bed. She thought she heard Steve coming into the room and then felt him sit down next to her. She felt her mother come to sit on her other side. She felt a hand on one shoulder, then a hand on the other, and then felt nothing but her own wrenching sobs.

"It's okay, Naomi. It's okay, now," Steve began.

Naomi's mother put her hand tentatively on her daughter's back as it jerked with silent sobs. After a while Naomi slowly sat up, and rested her head on her father's shoulder. Her body began to shake again with fresh sobs.

"You're okay." Steve wrapped his arm tightly around Naomi's shoulders.

The three sat in silence on Naomi's bed. Naomi kept her head down, trying to hide the tears but knowing that there was little reason to; what was happening was uncontrollable and Naomi knew it. Mei-mei was calling from the kitchen, indignant at being left alone for so long. Naomi felt her mother put her hand in her hair and gently place a fallen wisp behind her ear. "We'll talk about this later, sweetie," she said, then left the room.

Steve and Naomi continued to sit in silence. Steve spoke, "Whatever happened, Naomi, over there…we hope you'll tell us…eventually." There was another long pause as he reached for a tissue from a box beside Naomi's bed and handed it to his daughter. "But you know, your mother—both of us—need to understand why you would do such a thing…and especially not tell us. This is something we'll have to talk about when you're better. When you're ready."

Naomi nodded and blew her nose, grateful for Steve's understanding words. She was surprised by what had just happened, especially her own behaviour; she hadn't expected to burst into such a flood of tears. If anything, she had been preparing for a confrontation, and was ready to defend herself. For a second, Naomi was scared, all over again. *What's happening to me?*

The phone rang again, and Sara answered it after the first ring. "Hello?…Oh hello!" she said, surprised and pleased. "Yes, just a moment…she'll be happy to hear from you…Yes, she's…, okay. Hold on…Naomi!"

Bewildered, Naomi wiped her eyes with her fingers and looked up. "Thanks, Steve." she said, then headed to the kitchen. She took the phone from her mother, avoiding her gaze.

"Naomi?"

"Jovita!" Naomi gasped. "Hi!" She didn't know what else to say, too much was going on. She looked over at her mother, who was back at the table with Mei-mei and Steve. Naomi turned to face the wall.

"It's nice to hear from you," Naomi said, knowing that she didn't sound convincing.

"Naomi? Are you okay?" Naomi could sense her friend's concern in her voice, right through the phone line, and found herself trying hard to stifle another sob.

"I'm okay…uhhh…maybe you've heard—"

"Yes, Naomi…actually…that's why I'm calling…"

"Don't worry. We're a long way from Bali…sort of. We're all okay here. Looking forward to you coming for Christmas," Naomi said, and when she did, she knew, with a sinking feeling, what her friend was going to say next.

"Naomi…that's the thing…"

Naomi could tell her friend was almost in tears herself.

"My parents won't let me come now…I'm so sorry Naomi!"

"Oh…"

"I'm sorry Naomi, I really want to come. I want to be there with you."

Naomi leaned against the wall and squeezed the telephone receiver until it hurt, to stop the tears.

"…Mom says why don't you come here?" Jovita added.

Naomi straightened up, surprised by the invitation to spend Christmas back in Hong Kong, with Jovita and her family. For a fleeting moment she pictured herself at a big round table at some noisy Chinese restaurant with her best friend and her large wonderful family, and Naomi felt a little bit of happiness come back to her.

"That's sounds nice. But I couldn't. Sorry."

"Hmmm. Okay, Naomi. I understand. I know it's not the time to be leaving your family alone…Not now," Jovita replied, sympathetic but pragmatic, as always. Naomi heard Jovita sigh. "So…tell me about what's happening over there. Are you all okay? How's Mei-mei—?"

"Uh… Jovita," Naomi cut in. "Can I get back to you? I'll email you and tell you everything, okay?"

"Yes, sure…okay," Jovita replied. "Are you *sure* you're okay?"

"No," Naomi answered back. Her best friend wasn't coming now, and Naomi had been looking forward to showing her all over Lombok, her part of her beautiful new country. Her discovery. Disappointment welled up in Naomi, and she leaned against the wall to steady herself. Mike had promised Naomi he'd take them both for a flight over the island. *Why doesn't anything good happen any more?* Naomi thought. She squeezed the receiver once again, and dug her fingernails into her hand. She knew she was going to start to cry if something didn't change soon.

"Listen...Jovita? Don't worry about it. I have to go...I'll email you, okay? Bye." Naomi hung up the phone without waiting for her friend's goodbye. She turned around to face her parents. She saw that they were looking back at her with sorrowful expressions and in a way it made her annoyed, adding to the jumble of emotions she was feeling. Naomi wanted to just get away from everything.

"I know that we need to talk," she said, staring defiantly at her mother. "But not now...I'm going to the hotel to email Jovita like I said I would...okay?" She turned and fled out the back door before anyone else in the room had a chance to respond. As soon as she was outside, she ran through the trees to the beach. She fell onto the sand, wiping tears from her eyes with both her hands. She looked up and stared across to Bali and Gunung Agung though the mist, as she had done so many times before. She stared for a long time at the majestic peak, and thought of how, over there, on that island, things were so different now. Forever different now. Life had suddenly become a lot more difficult for people over there—and all over the country. Naomi continued to focus on the symmetry of the volcanic peak, and became slowly more aware of her breathing, and felt better as she tried to slow it down, to calm herself. *I sit here, and I feel a part of it. A part of the pain,* she thought. In a strange way, acknowledging this feeling made her feel better. *I am a part of this place.*

Naomi sat, for how long she didn't know, almost surprised that her mother hadn't come out to give her the talking-to that she knew was going to happen sooner or later. She got up and headed south along the beach, in the direction of the resort hotel. *I'll email Jovita, just like I said I would,* Naomi thought to herself. *I can't get into trouble for that!* She started to jog along the wet sand at the water's edge, happy to be feeling the wind in her hair, grateful to be doing something that was so simple, and yet for so many, like the people across the water, it was not something they could imagine doing right now—and for so many more everywhere, it was not something they could do or ever *would* do. Suddenly Naomi realized that she felt grateful, once again, just to be alive, to have the luxury of running free on a beautiful beach, in a beautiful place.

Naomi brushed the sand off her legs and sandals before heading into the business centre at the hotel. The staff at the reception desk smiled at her as they always did, although she knew they, too, were feeling that things were not at all business as usual. Naomi logged onto the computer and started browsing the website of the *Sydney Morning Herald*. She was dismayed to see the photo of a man sitting in a hospital bed, his face and head bandaged, and his eyes horribly swollen. There were cuts on his arms, and Naomi was horrified to read that they were shrapnel wounds, which so many of the injured were suffering from. Naomi shivered and began reading. Almost 200 people, mostly Australian tourists, along with many Indonesians who had been working at the bombed nightclub, had died. The nightclubs in the trendy area had all been full. There were at least 400 people in hospitals around Denpasar and Kuta and Sanur, and elsewhere. And almost two days later, there were still people unaccounted for, still buried under rubble. Naomi continued to scan the piece, and when she read that the police were calling the tragedy a suicide bombing by a group of Muslim extremists, she felt numb inside. *Why do they hate us?* Naomi found herself wondering again. *Why do they hate so much?*

Naomi clicked onto the *Jakarta Post*, scanning the photos of more injured people. She scrolled down, and another headline caught her attention under the banner *Breaking News. Rupiah Plummets.* With a sinking feeling, Naomi learned that, so far this morning, the Indonesian currency had gone down in value by another 10%.

"More bad news. I don't know how much more the people can handle," said a familiar male voice.

Naomi turned. Mike was standing there, his face bore a smile, but his eyes reflected his sadness and concern. She was surprised at how relieved she felt to see him.

"Mike," she began, and then, surprisingly, she could feel her mouth start to quiver. She felt horrified at the thought that she was going to start to cry in front of Mike, but was unable to stop it. "It's terrible—"

Mike put his arm around Naomi's shoulders and held her close. "It's bad. I know."

"My friend's not coming now," Naomi said in response. It sounded dumb to her and she felt embarrassed for saying it. *As if that matters when everything else is going wrong.*

"Ah, I see…" Mike patted Naomi's shoulder. "Well…that's too bad. Too bad for her. I can't blame the parents though. We'll have to find another excuse, then, for getting you up in my plane. I'll talk to Wahab and Farah; I'll ask if Noor wants to go—"

"Yes, that's good," replied Naomi.

Mike reached into his pocket and pulled out a worn handkerchief. He grinned and handed it to Naomi. "Don't worry. It's clean."

Naomi managed a smile for Mike's benefit, and accepted his offering.

13

tiga belas

"YOU SAY NOOR GAVE BLOOD? I didn't think Muslims did that" said Steve.

"Is that all you can say?" asked Sara reproachfully, trying to keep her anger under control. "Naomi went off to Bali, after that…that terrorist act. *And didn't tell us.* And you are thinking about what Muslims can or can't do?"

"I know this is none of my business. But what's done is done, Sara," Mike said. "I wouldn't worry about Naomi anyway, not with Noor—"

"Huh?" Naomi said indignantly. "Thanks for your support, Mike. You think I need Noor to lead me around?"

Mike laughed and raised his hands up defensively. "Well, I don't think you would have gone over to Bali on your own. But even if you had, I wouldn't worry about you. You seem to know what you're doing, I reckon—is what I'm saying." He turned to Sara and Steve. "You know, Naomi probably saved a life by donating blood. From what she told us, it was grave for a lot of people there."

"Thanks Mike. And you're right about Noor, though. It was his idea." For a moment Naomi thought about the man who had died in the chair next to her. She hadn't told her parents or Mike about him; she had told only Noor about it on the way back to Lombok. "Is it really true about Muslims not giving blood?" she asked, trying to change the subject. She felt she had done enough explaining for one day.

Mike answered, "Well, there are some basic principles, although there are different kinds of Muslim followers, some more conservative than others—"

"Like in any religion…even Methodist," said Steve.

Mike smiled at Steve's attempt at a joke. "But in this case, most Muslims, by far, would not have a problem with it. It was voluntary…and needed. Why don't you talk to Wahab about it, or ask Noor himself?"

Naomi nodded, "I think Noor is a kind of a…strict Muslim. More than the rest of his family, anyway."

Sara looked over at her daughter. "What makes you say that?"

Naomi remembered the conversation she and Noor had had by the waterfall when they were climbing Mount Rinjani. "Well, he seems to be more wary of foreigners."

"Well I can sure understand that. I've done my share of ferrying high-paying tourists around these parts," said Mike. "But I don't think that has anything to do with religion."

Steve chuckled at Mike's remark. "And Noor works as a guide at a posh resort, so I'll bet he's not seen the best of us. You know how it is Naomi, people from rich nations think they can come to poor countries with their money and throw it around. Act like they want without regard for the local people and their customs," Steve said, then added, "But you remember, Wahab told us about the problem of friends of the powerful here, buying up land, especially here in Lombok, and building these huge resort hotels and restaurants that are so expensive no local person could ever afford to go there—"

"I know. I know," said Sara, "but we're getting off the subject. We need to talk about our daughter. Naomi went and did something irresponsible. Giving blood was good. It's always good to help." Sara turned to Naomi. "And I'm proud of you for that, really I am. But to do it under these circumstances, and especially to mislead us about what you were doing…And now, Steve, you are suggesting we reward her with a flight over Lombok with Mike?"

Steve shrugged. "Naomi knows she didn't do the right thing. But why deny her this experience, Sara? That's not what we do. That's not why we're here. Is it?"

Sara looked around the table. "I know I'm outnumbered, but…I don't know, right now…I don't know. You're going to have to give me some time to think about it. I think a punishment is in order."

"Well, there's no rush. I'm off on a delivery for a couple of weeks, to Sulawesi. Just pigs and mail. Pigs and the post," said Mike.

"Will you be going back to Borneo anytime soon?" asked Naomi. She had always wanted to hear more about Mike's experiences there, but felt that he didn't want to talk. Now, after her own experience in Bali, she sort of felt she could understand why.

Mike stared into his coffee cup. "No… I don't think I'll be going back there for a while. I think I've done one too many rescue missions. Evacuating people who live under volcanoes is one thing, but saving one ethnic group from another—" he stopped, looked over at Naomi, and frowned. He drank down the last of his coffee. "Well…we'll see." Mike pushed back his chair and stood up. "That reminds me. I've got a few things to take care of before I go. Thanks for another lovely meal, Sara."

Naomi, Sara, and Steve walked Mike out the door to the gate and watched as he sauntered down the road towards Senggigi. Naomi felt the warm breeze on her skin and was tempted to grab Mei-mei and go for a swim at the beach. But, more than anything else at that moment, she wanted to make sure she could go flying with Mike and Noor. She looked over at her mother.

"Mom. What's up with Mike? I can tell you have a problem with him," Naomi said. She had liked Mike from the start, especially admiring his daring, and enjoying his straightforward manner. Naomi could tell that her mother did not share the same feelings.

Sara looked at Naomi and then at Steve. She frowned and shrugged her shoulders and waited, trying to figure out what to say. "I…I think Mike is…I think he's troubled. He's great, but he's got a lot held inside. I just hope he learns to take care of himself."

Steve nodded. "I know what you mean, Sara. He seems like the quintessential intrepid crazy pilot type…but I don't believe it myself," he replied. "If I ever saw what I know he's seen, I'd be in need of therapy, that's for sure. Look…he's flown enough dangerous missions in Borneo and also in Papau New Guinea to be considered a top-class bush pilot. That's got to be stressful—"

"Yeah but…I think what I really mean is that I sense he's on the edge…of something," said Sara. "I'm not sure what."

"You may be right. Mike lives life on the edge. Maybe for a guy like him, living a life more ordinary, like us, would make him die of boredom.

Some people are like that, right? They're not happy to live life on the sofa," Steve replied.

Naomi laughed. "We don't do that, either, do we? I agree that Mike is the kind of guy that needs to be where the action is. I admire that."

"From what he's done, he sounds like a real hero, too," said Sara.

Naomi reached over and grabbed her mother's hand. "So, Mom…please? Please can I go for a flight over Lombok with…a real hero?"

Sara looked over at her daughter and let out an exasperated sigh. "With Noor…okay," she said, finally relenting.

Yes! Naomi hit the air with her first. "I know Steve already asked Wahab, and he said it would be okay."

"I know you two will have an exciting time…Just do not go off on more heroic mission of your own, you hear?"

"Thanks Mom…Steve," Naomi cried out. She was relieved to be back in her mother's good books, but it was the idea of flying free over Lombok with Mike and Noor that made Naomi's heart jump for joy.

• • • • • •

"What do you mean?" asked Noor. Naomi realized she had just said something wrong.

"Nothing…I just mean that…I'm wondering why…You know…the suicide bombers in Kuta were Muslim. Why do Muslim people seem to always hate, you know, foreigners? First it was Nine Eleven…and now, the Bali Bombing. "

"That is the stupidest thing I ever heard!"

Naomi drew back, startled by Noor's increasingly angry response.

"You think you know—"

Naomi heard the reproach in his voice, and decided she didn't like it. "What's wrong with you? Everyone's saying it was an attack against foreigners. That's why it was in a nightclub frequented by *foreign tourists! And I know you don't like them!"* Naomi shot back defensively. "Or maybe they did it because Bali is a Hindu island…maybe that's why they did it. Hindus and not Muslims."

Noor's eyes narrowed at Naomi and he looked away, staring out the window for several moments before turning back to Naomi. "That's not true. But that's not even what I'm angry about!" Noor shouted. "You think this is what all the Muslim people think now, because everyone is saying it's Muslims—or Muslim *extremists! That's* all you think!" Noor shook his head in frustration. "They're not Muslims, Naomi…those terrorists. They're not *Muslim* terrorists. They're just *terrorists!"*

"But it's about Islam, isn't it? They say they are fighting a holy war—"

"So? You think this is what Islam is all about! You think you know all about Islam! You watch my sisters pray one morning, then you think you know! You say you enjoy the *music* coming from the mosques—and then you think you understand Islam!" Noor shot back, glaring at Naomi. "And then you say *I hate tourists. You know nothing about us…*You don't know anything about *me."*

Naomi could barely breathe as she listened to Noor speak. She was cringing at the energy that crackled in his anger. She pressed her fingers to her lips to stop them from trembling, and turned to look outside, trying to wipe a tear from her cheek in a way that wouldn't be detected. She'd done enough crying to last her a long time, she decided, but as she continued to listen to Noor, she felt for sure she had hit rock bottom.

"It's all the Muslims' fault. Blame Muslim people. Islam makes us hate—all around the world!" Noor shouted. "What about you? You *Christians.* I could say the same about you, but I'm not so stupid. *Babykillers."*

Naomi turned. "What are you talking about?"

Noor stopped. He eyed Naomi, and spoke in a voice heavy with sarcasm. "Oh you know, you Christians. Christians who talk about Babykillers. Christians who kill doctors—because they believe in the *sanctity of life—"*

Naomi shook her head, trying to understand the way the conversation was going. But now she just felt surprised. "How do you know about that?" she asked. She sniffed, brushed another tear from her cheek, and didn't care if Noor saw.

"Yes. Of course. You wonder how I know about such a thing. How would I know about that—me, a poor person from a poor country. How could I know about something that happens where you come from?…Yes, Naomi, I am a poor person, from a poor country," Noor said quietly, and then his voice rose, *"But I am not stupid!"*

Naomi felt the knot in her stomach tighten, and she thought she could feel Noor's anger towards her in his dark eyes. She felt that maybe Noor was right: *Maybe I don't know Noor at all.* Naomi buried her face in her hands. Noor was saying nothing now. She heard him sigh in a tired, frustrated way. Naomi wiped her nose on her sleeve and moved forward to reach for the door handle.

"Mike's coming." Noor said, as he handed his bandanna to Naomi.

"Hey kids, looks like we've got the green light—" Mike was clambering through his door and looked into the back seat. "Struth! What's going on here?"

Naomi was blowing her nose into Noor's bandanna. She looked up at Mike, unsmiling, and was surprised that she felt no embarrassment. The look of concern on Mike's face made her burst into tears once again. *Noor scares me…sometimes. I thought I was just starting to figure him out—*

Mike stared at Noor and Naomi, and back to Noor, shaking his head. "I don't know what's going on here—and I'm not asking you to tell me, either. You're both adults…well, pretty close, anyway…But I'll tell you this," he said. There was a pause. Naomi blew her nose and looked up at Mike, waiting to hear what he was going to say. "What can I tell you?" Mike muttered under his breath. A quiet giggle erupted from Naomi's throat. Mike smiled at her gratefully and patted her knee before raising a finger in the air. "I'll tell you this," he repeated. "Life's too short—" he began. Noor and Naomi were both waiting to hear more, but Mike hesitated, then said simply, once again, "Life's too short." He turned back in his chair. "Okay you guys, let's go for a ride. And let's forget whatever it is that's troubling us. Let's fly free from the *surly bonds* of *earth!* And as your father would say, Naomi…Tally Ho!" Mike finished in a mock British accent.

Naomi laughed out loud, grateful for Mike's mere presence as well as his sense of humour. She looked out her window, her back to Noor, determined to focus on what was outside the plane. She realized that she was embarrassed that Mike caught her and Noor having a blow-out argument, but not at the fact that he had seen her tears. The argument had been utterly unexpected; Naomi had been looking forward to this day for two weeks, had been dreaming of it; to fly over Lombok with Noor and Mike. Thinking of it had made the sadness of so many things slightly more bearable. But now, in the course of a conversation that had seemed so ordinary at first, at least to her, Naomi was now sitting next to Noor in stony silence. Naomi tried to figure out where the conversation had taken its unfortunate turn. She retraced her thoughts, replaying the conversation, and decided that Noor was the one who was out of line.

Suddenly Naomi decided she wanted to be far away from Noor; his anger had made her more than a little nervous, and the plane all of a sudden seemed too small for the three of them. As the plane began to taxi down the runway to the opposite end, Naomi focused on the small airport terminal building, and at the windsock next to it, which was showing, at that moment, that there was not much wind. She remembered what Mike had said during one of their many conversations about flying; that there's not very much wind in the tropics, but sometimes you needed it if you were running out of gas and you had to hope for tailwinds. *How many times has Mike been in danger himself?* Naomi wondered, trying to get her mind off of Noor.

Naomi leaned forward in her seat and turned to watch Mike at the controls. He seemed happy in his plane, she decided, the happiest she had seen him in all the short time she had known him. Naomi stared at Mike's profile, thinking that he was too preoccupied with the take-off procedure to realize he was being watched. But Mike turned in his seat and looked straight at Naomi, not noticing, or perhaps not caring that she had been watching him. "Seatbelts on, guys? We're ready to roll."

Naomi sat back in her chair, and within moments the aircraft was heading skyward, and Naomi's thoughts were lost in the beauty of the island. Mike headed north up to the Gili islands, and Naomi could see the fluorescent tropical colours of the reef and fish beneath the crystalline waters. Immediately Naomi was reminded of the day that Noor had taken her snorkelling there. *That was the day I think we became friends.* Naomi turned slightly in her seat, looked at Noor out of the corner of her eye and saw that his head was bowed against the window on his side of the plane. She couldn't see his face, and wondered what he was thinking, and if he was feeling as sad as she was. Mike circled the islands and then turned east in a deliberate angle. In a moment they were flying over the grand majestic beauty of Mount Rinjani. *We climbed that, Noor and me.*

Everything here reminds me of Noor, Naomi thought. She rested her head against the window and sighed. She wanted to turn to him and offer an apology, but she was sure he would refuse it. *He's so stubborn!* Naomi stared down at the lush green earth and marvelled at the pool of water found in the crater of the volcano, the most beautiful robin's-egg blue.

"Beauty...that is," Naomi could hear Mike say above the noise in the plane.

"It sure is," Naomi replied. Noor said nothing. "Let him stew, then," Naomi grumbled. *It's not my fault. Noor doesn't have to bite my head off for saying what I think.*

After 45 minutes Mike turned and headed back to the small airstrip. Naomi dreaded the moment when the plane's engines would be shut off; it had protected her from the silent treatment she and Noor were giving each other.

"Thanks, Mike, for the ride, it was fantastic," Noor said as Mike opened the passenger door. "I'm heading to the hotel—"

"Can I give you a lift?" Mike asked. Noor was already heading in the direction of the terminal building.

Noor looked over his shoulder, not breaking his stride. "Thanks, Mike, but I don't need it."

Mike shrugged and tuned back to Naomi. "Don't know what's eating him...but I'll bet you do, Naomi." There was a pause before he chuckled. "Don't tell me...and I won't ask. But remember what I said."

Naomi gave Mike a quick hug. "I know. Thanks for the ride, too, but I'll flag a donkey. I can't wait to tell Mom and Steve what I saw," she said, doing her best to sound cheerful. She could tell by the look on Mike's face that he was not convinced.

Naomi headed for the terminal, and began to think of what she could do to cheer herself up. *Maybe I'll stop at the market for a coconut juice. Maybe I'll stop by the school and see who's there.* By the time she had turned onto the street, Noor was already a long way down the road. Naomi wanted to run up to him and walk beside him, and hold his hand. She imagined them walking through the market together.

Life's too short, Mike had said, and Naomi had a feeling Mike knew what he was talking about. Naomi looked at Noor's receding figure and nodded. *I'll try again in a few days.*

14

It was a great holiday pageant at the school. We had a show combining both a Christmas celebration and the Muslim festival Idul Adha. I was surprised to discover just how much Christians and Muslims have in common. I almost didn't believe it when Jameela and Fathima told me that Jesus is mentioned in the Koran! The Koran also mentions Adam and Eve, Cain and Abel, Noah, David and Goliath—even Mei-mei's favourite story, Jonah and the Whale! Idul Adha commemorates the story of Abraham (Ibrahim in Arabic) and his son Ismael .

"NAOMI, I'VE GOT A SURPRISE FOR YOU. Let's just call it an early birthday present," said Steve as he entered the kitchen.

Naomi was sitting at the table, studying the geometric designs of the pineapple centrepiece in front of her, still dejected over her unfriendly parting with Noor the day Mike took them flying. Since that time Naomi had thought of little else, although it had been more than a week. She had put on an excited front for Mei-mei and her parents when she had come home that day, regaling then with her description of the Gili islands and Mount Rinjani from the air, as well as Mike's stomach-lurching turns, all in fun. She felt that she had done a good job of hiding her feelings, but it was exhausting work and Naomi was tired. Naomi looked up at Steve. He seemed so excited that Naomi had to smile.

"You're going to *New York City!*"

Naomi stared.

"It was a trip that all of use were supposed to make. I had meetings in New York, but…due to the situation…the meetings on my project have been cancelled. And I have to sit tight for now."

Slowly Naomi turned to look at Steve. *Was this for real?* Sara came up behind Steve and beamed at Naomi.

"I'd bought tickets for you and your mother and Mei-mei, as a surprise. So, now it looks like you are going without me—"

"Whoa…Steve. What a surprise!" Naomi threw herself into Steve's arms, almost knocking him over, then turned to give her mother a big hug as well.

"But…Mom…what about the school?"

"Well…Farah and I have decided to extend our New Year break. We'll start up the school again in February. I think we could use it, don't you?" asked Sara.

Naomi nodded, knowing what her mother was referring to. Since the Bali bombing, many people had lost their jobs, not just in Bali, but in Lombok as well. And the devaluation of the rupiah had made matters worse. The mothers of the young students had said they would not be re-enrolling their children after the break, and a couple of the adult students, whose lessons were being paid for by their employers, were also forced to withdraw as a cost-cutting measure.

"At least we had a chance to have a great Christmas party," said Naomi. "And *Idul Adha.*"

Sara returned her daughter's embrace, "That's my girl."

Naomi felt demoralized, but knew she should be grateful for having something new and exciting to think about, for the time being. *It's strange how these things keep coming,* Naomi thought to herself. *Even when bad things happen, there's always good things happening, too—for me, anyway.*

"Dad, I can't wait. When do we leave?"

"Monday. Is that soon enough?" Steve joked.

Monday was just three days away. It was too soon! But the more Naomi thought of it, the more excited she felt. Then, briefly, she thought of Noor and the fact that it seemed they were no longer friends. Naomi had not mentioned this to her parents. *Maybe a little time away is exactly what I need,* Naomi thought.

"I hardly have time to pack!"

• • • • • •

That's New York below me! Naomi thought. The jumbo jet was circling over the city on its approach to Newark International Airport in New Jersey, and the sky was clear and bright—perfect for viewing the awesome sight.

Naomi turned to her mother, who had lifted the sleeping Mei-mei from her seat next to Naomi to exchange seats. Sara, too, was craning her neck to get a good view of New York City. Naomi giggled, "How many times have we been like this: you and me with our faces crunched up against an airplane window, trying to see the place we're going to?"

"Hmm, let's see: There was Tokyo, Vancouver—in transit only, though—Hong Kong, Beijing, Jakarta—"

"Couldn't see much there. It was dark—"

"True. There was Lombok—" Sara continued.

"Ha!" Naomi interrupted, laughing. "There's not much to see—"

"You surprise me!" Sara interjected. "I know you love all that lovely green—and blue. Those rice fields. The volcano? That's pretty something."

Naomi nodded, "Yeah, you're right. But I meant big cities. Like this one. You look down and see how unbelievable it is. What we have done. All that—humanity," Naomi finished, at a loss how to really explain what she was feeling and thinking.

Naomi turned her attention back to the window. She was able to clearly see the island of Manhattan tapering to a point at its southern end, and the dense conglomeration of skyscrapers. Naomi knew where the World Trade Center had been located, at the southern end of that Island. Naomi was looking for something, and her eyes stopped searching when she could see a grey square shape discernible among the tightly-packed buildings. Naomi wondered if it was Ground Zero. She felt certain she was right. A shiver ran through her. The clean-up process had been going on for many weeks now. Naomi knew not all the missing had been found, and that some bodies would forever remain unaccounted for. *People had been obliterated here, just like at Hiroshima,* Naomi thought. *But not people's memories of them.* She thought of Sadako, the young girl in Hiroshima who had died from leukemia 10 years after the nuclear bomb was dropped on her city. Today, people from all over the world still thought about her, and read about her, and sent paper cranes to the Hiroshima Peace Park to let her spirit know they still remembered and cared.

Naomi's thoughts continued to linger on Japan, the first place she had lived outside of Canada, when she was 12 years old. She thought of the physical beauty of the place, and the destruction caused by the Hiroshima bombing. She had seen the evidence when she visited that city. Naomi's thoughts turned to Bali—another place of unequalled beauty, scarred by an act of hate. The Bali bombing was still fresh in Naomi's mind. In this case, the missing had all been accounted for now. More than two hundred people had been killed, and many more injured. Those numbers were less than in New York City, where three thousand people had died. But that one statistic did not lessen the horror and the pain for anyone.

Naomi felt her eyes suddenly prick with tears, and she wiped them quickly with her finger, hoping her mother wasn't watching her. *Hiroshima, New York City, Bali. What had those people ever done?* And then, as if in response, Naomi recalled the man in Bali, dying next to her, and the last words he had uttered: *I didn't do anything.* Naomi could hear his laboured breathing and the words in her mind all over again. *What did he mean?* Naomi wondered once more. She realized she had often found herself thinking about the man, wondering what those final words had meant. Naomi tried to understand why he had to be injured, why he had to be killed, and why, perhaps, someone felt he had deserved such pain and suffering. Naomi continued to contemplate the man's final words. Maybe he knew he was going to die, and, in his final moments, he had decided that he could have done more. Maybe, in his final moments—if he knew that's what they were—he had been lamenting the things he had not done in his life.

"Naomi, are you okay?" Sara asked.

Naomi turned to her mother. "I'm okay. I was just—thinking." She realized she had been holding her breath, thinking again about the man in the tent. She looked at her mother sheepishly; she knew that her mother would have been expecting a better answer than that. But instead, her mother pointed out the window and leaned forward again. "See that? The Statue of Liberty."

"Naomi squeezed in close to her mother. "Where? Oh there! Yes! I see it. Wake up Mei-mei."

Sara laughed. "I don't think so. She's our baby, and she's never heard of New York City. And she's going to stay sleeping just as long as she can."

Naomi nodded, then thought about Steve, back in Lombok. She knew he would be missing them all. Naomi wished Steve were with them, so they could experience this New York adventure as a family. But she also knew that Steve's job was becoming more complicated. The events in Indonesia were causing problems for the project Steve was working on; some people felt the project could not continue—not when the country's economy was in such trouble. It seemed unfair to Naomi that Steve's water sanitation project could be in jeopardy, when huge hotels and airports were still being planned. Some people, like Noor, felt that building a new airport on Lombok was a mistake altogether, because it would change Lombok for the worse; displacing hundreds of peasant families who farmed the land. It would also turn the island into what Bali had become; one of the world's most beautiful spots was now a place of wall-to-wall restaurants and shops, where the streets were clogged with traffic, and where children had learned to beg and even steal on the beaches.

Bali is still beautiful, though, Naomi thought. *Despite what Noor thinks.* Noor. Naomi pictured his face, she pictured him sitting next to her on the hovercraft heading back to Lombok, the day they had gone to Bali to donate their blood. On that day, Naomi had felt a bond. Then Naomi pictured Noor walking away after their flight with Mike, and the argument they'd had in the plane. Suddenly Naomi regretted not calling him to say goodbye. An ache rose up in Naomi's chest. *I miss him. Maybe I'll call him*, Naomi thought. *No, that would surprise him too much. He probably wouldn't like it,* Naomi decided. *I'll send him a postcard.*

•   •   •   •   •   •

"Where to first, Mom?" Naomi asked, bouncing on the bed as soon as they arrived at the hotel.

Mei-mei giggled and put out her arms. "Lift me up, Naomi," she said.

Naomi lifted her little sister into her arms and together they fell back onto the mattress, giggling. Sara looked over at her daughters playing on the bed. "We have five days to explore. That should give us just about enough time to see the Statue of Liberty, the Metropolitan Museum of

Art, Central Park, Times Square, the United Nations complex, a walk down Fifth Avenue—"

"Is that where all the good shopping is?" asked Naomi. She wasn't exactly sure what good shopping was in New York, although she had heard of stores named Neiman Marcus, Macy's, Bloomingdales, and Tiffany's. It had been a long time since Naomi had been into the fancy shops of Hong Kong's Central District, but she knew, also, that this was not something she missed, living in Lombok.

"Yes, we can go window shopping. We can have breakfast at Tiffany's, just like Audrey Hepburn did. A croissant and a latte while we walk down the street," Sara replied. She and Naomi laughed together at the thought.

"And we'll have to go to a show on Broadway. I'm sure they must have something for kids. We'll take Mei-mei to Chinatown over on the east side. And we'll have to go to the Empire State Building, for the view—" Naomi was sitting up on the bed, holding her sister in her lap. She and her mother looked at each other, both were thinking the same thing: had things been different, they would be taking an elevator to the top of one of the World Trade Center's twin towers. It was not only for the unequalled view, but to experience a major wonder of the modern world; to be on top of what had been, for so long, the tallest building in the world. It was strange, and sad, to think that it had been vanished.

"…That'll be good," Naomi replied.

Sara spoke. "Okay, shower and then let's go. I've already asked at the front desk about bus tours of the city. That's what we'll do today," she said, "Unless, of course, the jet-lag is catching up with you—"

Naomi shook her head. "I'm still okay. It's only early afternoon. Let's try to keep Mei-mei up and then we can all relax here after dinner."

"Good idea."

Later, the three headed downstairs and waited in the hotel lobby for the tour bus to arrive. Naomi noticed that there were several people waiting, and it struck her how different they all looked from other people in the lobby; those who were obviously at the hotel on business of some kind. Those people, men and women, seemed more solemn, preoccupied maybe, and were more smartly dressed. They walked more quickly, too, and never seemed to be looking around, but were, instead, always looking where they were going. It seemed to Naomi that black and navy clothing was the uniform of these bustling city people. Naomi looked down at her shirt under her bright purple coat, with its traditional Indonesian batik design. Naomi continued to watch the businesspeople come and go through the hotel lobby, she wondered how they were feeling; if they were still thinking about Nine Eleven and still feeling it effects. She wondered how it had affected them personally. She watched a young, impeccably dressed brunette cross the marble floor and in her mind Naomi asked: *Do you know anyone who died? Did you watch the towers fall? Are you all right now? Are you afraid? How brave you are to be here after the horror.*

Through the hotel doors, Naomi could see a tour bus idling just outside. Naomi helped Mei-mei to her feet and joined the line to get on the bus, excited about seeing the city. As the bus moved along the east side of Manhattan, the tour guide pointed out the monolithic, rectangular-shaped building behind a row of flags. Naomi knew that this was the headquarters of the United Nations. She and her mother and Mei-mei would be going there tomorrow, to meet with some other employees on overseas postings, along with their families. As the bus drove by, Naomi craned her neck to look at the flags of all the member-nations. Canada's red and white flag popped out at her easily. She giggled when she realized it was actually the red and white stripes of the Indonesian flag.

Over three hours, the bus had taken them from one end of Manhattan Island to the other, from Battery Park at the southern end, looking out over the Statue of Liberty and Staten Island beyond it, through the Wall Street financial district and then on to Times Square. The tour guide was especially animated when the bus drove down Broadway, and she pointed out the various theatres where famous people had gotten their first big break, and where all the sold-out shows were now playing, naming several of them. Naomi was reminded once again how little she knew about what was popular and fashionable in North America. She had lived in Canada for only one year in the past six. *I've spent almost all my teenage years in Asia,* Naomi thought. She smiled, realizing that the idea made her feel proud of herself, and her mother—and her whole family.

As the bus made its way along with the rest of the traffic on Fifth Avenue, the guide pointed out shops and buildings that Naomi had heard of: Tiffany's, Neiman Marcus, the Trump Tower. They passed by the Empire State Building. The tour guide explained that it had been the tallest building in New York City and the world when it was built in 1931, and that, now, it was once again the tallest building in New York City. Upon hearing this, the passengers became subdued. Once again, Naomi knew that many of the passengers were thinking the same thing. The guide explained that the area where the twin towers had once stood was still off limits. Much of the southern tip of the island was still closed off to non-residents. The tour was far too quick, it seemed to Naomi, but she had a good idea of Manhattan now, and where the hotel was situated among all the sights. The passengers were invited to get off the bus at its last stop, the Metropolitan Museum of Art. Naomi looked at her mother hopefully, but Sara took one look at a sleepy Mei-mei in her lap and looked apologetically at Naomi. "Don't worry," Sara said. "There's always tomorrow."

Naomi nodded and looked out at the museum, struck by its sheer size. There was nothing as big as that in Lombok. She had forgotten how big things could be. Even so, Naomi admired the building and what it represented; a place where people could seek peace, and a monument to people's creativity.

When Naomi opened the door to her hotel room, she saw that the telephone message light was blinking. She lifted the receiver and the operator explained that there was a message for her mother, and that she would have to come to the desk and pick it up personally. "It's a message from someone named Dale. I don't know who that is," Sara said, puzzled, when she returned to the room. She sat down on the bed and dialled the number, and Naomi heard her mother introduce herself, and then listen to the speaker. Naomi watched her mother's face go from surprise to delight, to an expression she couldn't quite fathom. *What is she talking about!* Naomi was dying to find out.

"…Yes…Do you think so? Would it be all right?…Well, of course! Oh my…Okay…we'll be waiting in the lobby at seven o'clock tomorrow morning…Thank you, Dale." She turned to Naomi slowly, as if she couldn't believe herself what plans she had just made. "Naomi, that was a woman from the United Nations. She actually used to be posted to the field in Indonesia years ago, she said." Then Sara stopped and shook her head, her eyes widened, "Dale said that she was able to plan a special visit for us tomorrow. We're going to Ground Zero."

15

lima belas

THE NEXT MORNING, AFTER A QUICK BREAKFAST, Naomi and her mother and sister headed to the lobby, eager to start their day. Despite the early hour, another family was already sitting together on a sofa in the lobby, clearly waiting for someone—or something—to happen. Minutes later, a middle-aged woman stepped out of a white minivan that had just pulled up to the hotel entrance. As the woman entered the lobby, she smiled at the family seated on the sofa, and then at Sara and Naomi. "Traffic is good this morning. I'm not late, am I?" she laughed. "Hello, I'm Dale Wheeler. You must be the Da Silvas, and you," she said, grinning at Naomi, "Must be our UN family from Indonesia." The two families drew close to Dale, while she made the introductions. "Nice to meet you all. Follow me, let's get going before the traffic wakes up. New York traffic is world famous…although perhaps you've seen worse where you've been posted."

Naomi held Mei-mei's hand, led her onto the minivan and chose the first row, wanting to make sure she got a good view. Sara and Mrs. Da Silva took the seat behind them, with her husband and two children occupying the back seat. Naomi listened as the two women quickly exchanged information: Mrs. Da Silva had been with the United Nations for almost 10 years, and was presently working for the World Health Organization, developing and implementing AIDS awareness programs in Mumbai. "How fascinating," Naomi heard her mother say. "You've got quite a task…" She went on to explain that her husband was involved with a water and sanitation project in Lombok, with the UN Development Program.

As they continued to talk, Naomi learned that Mrs. Da Silva had already been posted to Sri Lanka and Egypt. Naomi was impressed and awed by this intrepid person. She wondered how Mrs. Da Silva could be all that, and a mother, too.

Dale sat down next to the driver, then turned to face the passengers behind her. "Welcome to New York City," she said. "You're quite lucky that we have a small group today. Larger groups—even though we are with the UN—are not always granted entry into the Ground Zero site. I always make enquiries to visit the site when I am arranging visits to the UN for staff and their families here in New York, but the answer is usually 'No.' We got lucky today."

"Why do you think we got lucky?" asked Mrs. Da Silva.

Dale shrugged. "Well, as you may have guessed, Ground Zero is a busy place. Not just with all the people involved in the clean up and reconstruction work, but because people from all over—as well as from New York City—want to see it for themselves, and pay their respects. There are visitors every day—a lot of VIPs; visiting dignitaries from across the country and from overseas…even movie stars." Dale's smile widened. "So…to answer your question, maybe there is no 'big name' visiting at the moment. You can imagine it's a very secure place, but it gets even more so if there is someone major—"

"Well, that is lucky for us, then," Sara said.

Twenty minutes later, the minivan stopped at a blockade of large white fibreglass pylons, behind which a barricade of wire fencing and plywood had been erected. Naomi could see that a soldier was stationed there, writing down the licence number of their vehicle, with its special United Nations plate. The driver of the minivan showed his identification, and Dale asked everyone to hand over their passports for inspection. The soldier dutifully marked all these down on his clipboard. Then, slowly, the minivan moved forward and came to a stop in a makeshift parking lot. Dale got off and motioned for others to follow her to a prefabricated building. Everyone signed in and was given a hardhat, and then lead about 100 metres to a viewing area fashioned behind a low concrete barrier. "We can't stay long, 15 minutes only, I'm afraid," Dale told the group.

Naomi's eyes were drawn upwards as she approached the viewing area. There, all around her were the skyscrapers of Manhattan—those that had not been destroyed. An American flag was draped on one of the buildings: it was the largest flag Naomi had ever seen. Her eyes were drawn to it, its pristine red, white, and blue beaming amid what seemed a dusty greyness all around it. To Naomi, this American flag was a symbol of the people's wish to show the perpetrators they were unafraid; a dramatic and effective show of defiance.

Naomi saw a jumble from the corner of her eye; something was not right. She forced herself to follow it and was disturbed by what she saw. Her eyes rested on a huge tangle of steelwork, crumpled and pitched in an unlikely, precarious position. The broken shafts of the frame pointed up and outwards in a menacing way. Naomi knew it had been the decorative framework of one of the fallen buildings, but now it was a grotesque monument to the horror of what had happened to the world several months ago. Naomi couldn't breathe. Her blood ran cold as she stared at the wreckage. She surveyed the area, and could see that efforts were being made to remove the wreckage and that it was turning out to be an especially dangerous and daunting task.

As difficult as the job seemed to everyone, Naomi knew that, one day, there would be nothing left of the place but an empty pit, and then the task of rebuilding would begin. *But how can these people begin to rebuild their lives?* Naomi asked herself. Naomi remembered reading about many babies who were being born in the city, babies whose fathers had died on September 11th. *How would their families be rebuilt in the years to come?* Naomi wondered sadly. *Glad it's not me,* Naomi allowed herself to think. She brushed a tear from her cheek and turned to her mother, wondering what she was thinking. The group was silent as they looked out over the sight.

"We must leave now," Dale said after several more minutes. She led the group back to the prefab to return their hardhats. It was a sombre ride along the east side of Manhattan Island towards the complex of buildings that housed the headquarters of the United Nations. Naomi looked out at the East River, anticipating the guided tour that Dale had arranged for them. Steve had spoken of it before; he had visited the place years ago as a tourist, and of course Naomi had seen the large General Assembly Hall many times on television. A bridge came more closely into view, and once again Naomi felt a sense of recognition that jarred and unnerved her. It was the Brooklyn Bridge. Naomi remembered seeing it on television on the day of their arrival in Jakarta.

Except that, on that day, and at that time, there had been no vehicular traffic; the bridge had been filled with people crossing on foot. Naomi remembered how odd it had seemed at the time, the flood of people on that bridge, and the sad realization that it was an exodus from the terror that was unfolding on Manhattan. Naomi stared at the bridge for a long time.

"I was posted to Indonesia years ago," Naomi heard Dale say to her mother. "It was my second posting. I spent much of my time in Indonesian Borneo, working for UNIFEM."

Sara asked, "Have you ever been to Lombok?"

"No, I haven't," Dale replied. "Although I have been told countless times that I should go there, before it turns into another Bali. Actually, I haven't been back to Indonesia in over ten years, but I am still very interested in what's going on there. There's always something, as I'm sure you know," she added, her voice becoming a little hushed. "I was there shortly after Wirano took over. And it does look like things have come full circle for him—or will be, shortly."

"That's what my husband thinks," Naomi heard her mother say in a low voice. After a pause, Sara asked, "Do you suppose what happened in the Philippines could happen in Indonesia?"

"You mean 'People Power'? Good question. Indonesia and the Philippines are not the same," Dale said thoughtfully. "But, one should never underestimate the power of the people—and there are a lot of people in Indonesia." Naomi could tell Dale was smiling.

But Sara's hushed reply betrayed her concern. "Yes, I agree. The rupiah is in bad shape and it is going to get worse. You know, to tourists, it always sounds good; we have more left over to buy souvenirs. We don't see what hardship such a thing causes to people living there," she said. "And there have been riots already—not to mention the bombing in Bali." Sara was speaking so quietly now Naomi could hardly hear, and she turned her head a little in order to hear more clearly what her mother was saying. "I think that's why Steve was so keen have us come here to New York City, to get away from all that. But no one knows when it could happen again…and I'm starting to worry."

"You know, Sara, these conditions are always monitored by our offices. I can assure you that the safety of our field staff and their families our topmost concern. We don't leave our staff vulnerable in order to score political points—"

"That's good to hear. This is Steve's first posting with the UN. We're new to this."

By now Naomi was on alert. She didn't realize just how nervous her mother had become about being in Indonesia. Not since Nine Eleven. She had said nothing like that, even after the bombing in Bali. Naomi felt a little put off by the fact that her mother had not shared these feelings, but had just done so with a woman they had met only that morning. Naomi wondered how many times her mother and Steve had talked about this. Naomi remembered the joke Steve had made about being in Indonesia: he had said that it could be exciting, like in the movie Jovita had sent her, *The Year of Living Dangerously.*

It's not funny at all when it is real life, Naomi thought. *There is so much fear.* She had come to New York filled with excitement, and also, she had to admit, more than a bit of nervousness. But now, after seeing the people of New York City going on with their lives, they gave her a feeling of strength. As the minivan neared the UN headquarters, Naomi scanned the long lines of flags. It was, to her, a symbol of unity, and Naomi felt buoyed by this thought, and protected by the strength these flags and the building behind them represented. *Don't be afraid, Mom,* she said silently to her mother. *We'll be okay. Nothing will happen to us.*

The minivan made its way into a parking area near United Nations Plaza, and they walked towards the flags, stopping to take pictures in front of them. Naomi posed with her mother and Mei-mei while Mr. Da Silva took a photo, and she wished that Steve were there. In the main building Dale introduced them to a university student named Mudiwa, from Zimbabwe, who was working as an intern and, from what Naomi could tell, enjoying it very much. Naomi studied Mudiwa as the young woman led the tour, and began to imagine what this young woman's life must be like, living in New York and working for the United Nations.

At the end of the tour, Mudiwa took the group inside the great hall where the UN General Assembly convened. The hall was empty, and Naomi and the others were thrilled to be able to walk freely through the room, up and down the aisles. Naomi looked around the vast space in awe. She looked up at the podium, and then turned to the rows of seats, scanning the plates that bore the names of all the member-countries. Naomi looked up and smiled at the Da Silva children as they tried to squeeze into the chair reserved for the Sri Lankan representative. Mudiwa's laughter rang through the hall before Mrs. Da Silva's stern look told her boys that it was time to act their age.

"That's the tour, everyone. I hope you enjoyed it," said Mudiwa finally, and grinned at the applause she was given by the group. Naomi thought Mudiwa was joking when she mentioned that the gift shop was open, but was pleased to discover that it was true; the United Nations headquarters boasted a gift boutique selling an array of common souvenir items: pins and T-shirts, as well as various books about the history of the United Nations and its endeavours. Naomi came across a selection of postcards and began to browse through the rack, remembering that she wanted to send Steve one. Naomi grinned at the idea of sending a postcard to her Saturday morning students at Kartini's School—then reminded herself that Kartini's School was closed indefinitely. Naomi paused before selecting a postcard for them anyway. *We will reopen,* she said to herself.

Again, Naomi wondered if she should send a postcard to Noor as well. She wondered if he was hoping to get one. *Is he checking his mailbox and wishing for a surprise?* Naomi pushed the thought out of her head; convinced that it was nonsense. Many of the postcards were of United Nations Plaza, with the flags in front, or the General Assembly Hall. But there were also postcards with men's faces on them. One of them she knew was the present Secretary-General, but the others looked unfamiliar to her, and some of the black-and-white portraits looked rather dated. She picked up one postcard, of a handsome man with dark hair, and flipped it over. It was Dag Hammarskjöld, a former UN secretary general, from Sweden. *How does someone get to be Secretary-General of the United Nations?* Naomi wondered.

Naomi stopped to look at the portrait of another man, with thick black-framed eyeglasses and Asian features. Naomi picked the card from the rack and flipped it over: *U Thant. Burma, Secretary-General of the United Nations 1961-1971.* Naomi looked at the name and wondered. *U Thant. Is that his first name? U? How do you pronounce that?* She grinned and glanced up, looking for her mother, then turned to look down the aisle and saw that she was at the other side of the shop with Mei-mei.

Naomi grinned as an idea flashed through her mind. It was Steve's birthday in two weeks. Naomi picked up the postcard of U Thant, then grabbed another three off the shelf; pictures of the United Nations Plaza, for Jovita, her grandparents, and, Naomi decided, not for Noor alone, but for his whole family.

"You know you can mail these from here and the postcards will have a United Nations postmark," the salesperson said as she entered the purchases into the computer. "So you'll be wanting stamps then." The woman took five stamps from a drawer and added them in, then pointed to a table nearby where people were writing postcards and letters.

Naomi took her postcards and walked to the table, and was almost giggling as she fished for a pen from her bag. She turned over the postcard of U Thant. *Dear Steve, Happy Birthday to You, From U.* As she addressed the postcard to Steve in Lombok, Naomi's giggles bubbled over, and the visitors nearby looked at her and smiled. Naomi hurried out of the store and sat on the bench just outside, waiting for her mother and Mei-mei to finish their shopping. She was thinking of Steve and starting to giggle more loudly. *Steve will get the joke. Steve will love it. If that is the only thing I get for Steve for his birthday, it will be enough.* Naomi put her hand to her mouth, trying not to laugh, but then let go and laughed long and hard, looking forward to being back in Lombok with Steve. She couldn't wait to see the smile on his face.

16

enam belas

I really enjoyed visiting the UN headquarters. When we were walking up and down the aisles in the General Assembly Hall, I felt that the room was important, because it is where the world gets together—it's hard to explain. Mudiwa, our guide from Zimbabwe, says she is going to be UN Secretary-General someday. I believe her. It's interesting to listen to Mrs. Da Silva talk about her work, too. I think it would be cool to work for the United Nations.

"MOM. DALE'S ON THE PHONE," Naomi whispered. She didn't want to wake up the sleeping Mei-mei lying next to her. It was late afternoon, and Naomi and her mother were also feeling tired after their tour to Ground Zero and to the UN headquarters earlier in the day.

Sara took the phone. "Hello, Dale. Thanks again for the wonderful tour this morning…Of course! We'd love you to join us in Chinatown." Naomi looked over at her mother, who was looking back at her, beaming. Naomi could tell that she and Dale had really hit it off. She had heard her mother mention to Dale about how Mei-mei had become a part of the family, and how they were planning to take Mei-mei to New York's Chinatown. It had been a long time since Mei-mei had seen the familiar sights of her Chinese heritage back in Hong Kong. New York's Chinatown was, of course, not Hong Kong—but it would do nicely.

When Dale returned to the hotel, they took a taxi back to the southern end of Manhattan. Chinatown was a neighbourhood as busy as the rest of Manhattan, except for the area around Ground Zero, which seemed eerie without the bustle of New Yorkers getting on with the day. Naomi looked around her as she stepped out of the cab, holding Mei-mei's hand tightly. Right away, she noticed that Chinatown, too, had been affected by the destruction of the World Trade Center. The neighbourhood was, in fact, only a few blocks away from Ground Zero. Some buildings, especially on the upper floors, still had telltale dark patches; the remnants of the dust clouds that had enveloped the area on September 11th. Other buildings were pristine looking, and Naomi guessed that someone must have had the funds to pay for their cleaning.

After taking in the buildings of Chinatown, Naomi's eyes and ears—and nose—were drawn down to street level. Naomi was surprised at how this New York neighbourhood was strikingly familiar to her; almost as if a bit of Mongkok or Shamshuipo, in the heart of the Kowloon side of Hong Kong, had been transplanted into this corner of Manhattan. The signage, the produce, the many other items for sale, seemed to spill out of the shops and onto the sidewalks. Naomi looked down at her little sister and was pleased to see the look of wonder on her face. Mei-mei's eyes were wide as she surveyed the scene around her. Naomi kept watch, waiting for the smile that she knew would follow. The little girl grinned and clapped her hands with joy. Sara and Dale laughed, delighted at the pleasure the little Chinese girl was taking in being in a place that was once again familiar to her.

As the four walked down the street, Naomi's head swivelled from one side of the street to the other, her nose detecting scents that were at once familiar but also, it seemed, from a time in her past. Her mother was thinking the same thing.

"I think the sense of smell is the most evocative, don't you Dale?" Naomi heard her ask. "For me, this place brings back memories of my life in Hong Kong."

Naomi continued her stroll down the crowded street, holding her little sister's hand. *What kinds of things make us remember the cherished bits of our past?* Naomi thought. Naomi knew that, just like her mother and Mei-mei, walking through these streets brought Hong Kong back to her; the signs in Chinese, and also in English, so crowded in Hong Kong that they juggled for space over the streets, often jutting out well into the middle of the road overhead. Naomi looked at the display tables of exotic fruits in front of the shop they were passing. The fruity, ripe smell was also familiar, and with a smile Naomi scanned the heavily-laden tables looking for the source of the particularly pungent odour that was overpowering all the others.

"Look," Naomi said, pointing to several large, spiky-looking fruits that were resting at the back of one of the tables.

"Durian!" cried Mei-mei. She gasped and stretched out her hands, sniffing the air in one long, in-drawn breath. She was on tiptoes trying to reach it, and then, as if confused, she looked up at Naomi. She set her heels back on the sidewalk, and she grimaced.

Naomi laughed. "You forgot you don't like durian, didn't you, Mei-mei? Come on. Let's run!"

Mei-mei nodded silently, and Naomi grabbed her hand and together they tried to catch up to her mother and Dale, who were already half a block ahead. Naomi was giggling; Mei-mei had been so thrilled to see and smell the familiar fruit, beloved by many across Asia. But it seemed she had forgotten just how overpowering the smell could be. Durian was often referred to as 'King of the Fruit,' and although it is enjoyed for its taste, the intriguing thing about durian was that it smelled dreadful to many.

Naomi came up behind her mother, ready to tell her about Mei-mei's amusing reaction to rediscovering durian, but something stopped her cold. Dale was talking, and Sara was clearly upset.

"There has been several cases of isolated unrest in Indonesia: in Aceh, Sulawesi. Our field officers are monitoring the situation carefully. There are several things going on, at the same time, it seems; the rupiah's slide is seen as the main factor."

"And I know that there have been ethnic clashes," said Sara glumly. "In Borneo."

"And Sulawesi," added Dale.

Naomi saw her mother nod. "And Wirano has been in power for too long, probably."

Dale nodded. "You're right, And what often happens when an old dictator feels threatened…He'll bring in the troops. And that's what has happened yesterday in Jakarta, Sara. There was a demonstration of students at one of the universities. They were demanding Wirano's resignation. A student was killed by the police," Dale said. Naomi heard her mother gasp.

After a pause, Dale continued. She spoke quietly. "There was looting in Jakarta as well, and destruction of property in several Chinese neighbourhoods across the city…"

Naomi held Mei-mei's hand tighter.

"…If the situation deteriorates any further…I have done a bit of checking around with some colleagues. Things are worse than I thought. I hate to say it, but there is a very good chance that your husband's project—will definitely not got through."

Sara shook her head. Her voice cracked with emotion. "It's terrible—"

Dale looked at Sara and nodded. "It happens. It happened before. We get our people out. That is the bottom line. We get out, abandon the project until the time comes when we can return and finish the job. Sometimes it takes a long time. A new government, maybe. Sometimes it doesn't happen at all."

Naomi held her breath as she listened to what Dale was telling her mother. A wave of anxiety swept through her. She could see her mother's head bent in thought, her lips set, grim with worry. Naomi wondered what mental calculations her mother was making. Naomi knew she was thinking of Steve, and also thinking of the people in Lombok who were going to lose the water sanitation project they needed very much.

"But, but there's always a warning of things to come. Isn't there? You always knows what's going on…right?"

Dale replied slowly, "Some places are like, you know, pressure cookers, ready to boil over. In some ways, Indonesia has been like that for a long time. But it seems that even more things are being added into the mix. Economic difficulties—all the Asian economies are not doing too well at the moment—instability within the Muslim community—"

"Yes, I know," said Sara. "I've got friends there who have spent a lot of time trying to explain it all to me."

"And let's not forget the fear of more terrorist attacks," said Dana. "I can tell you, it's a strong fear—"

"I know," Sara said softly.

Dana put her hand on Sara's arm, "I'm sorry…of course you do." And then she added. "Add this to long-time unrest, the fight for independence in East Timor, and, maybe, the last, final grasp of a dictator who is losing touch with his people. It's an explosive mix." She stopped to look Sara in the eyes. "Does the UN always know when it's time to pull out? No, not always."

At that moment, Sara turned around and was surprised to see Naomi and Mei-mei so close behind her. She looked hard at Naomi, and Naomi knew she was wondering how much of the conversation Naomi had heard. Naomi grinned, determined that she wasn't going to give her mother more to worry about.

"Mom, we found some durian. Mei-mei was so happy to see it, she almost wanted to have a bite—until she remembered that she hated the stuff."

"Oh, really, " Sara said, sounding clearly distracted. "That's nice."

"Well, we're here," Dale said, striding ahead a few paces and opening the door of what appeared to be a traditional-looking Chinese-style tea house. "Dim sum for everyone!"

"Dim sum!" Mei-mei shouted with joy, thrilled to be getting a familiar treat, and for the rest of their time together, Sara, Naomi and Dale tried hard to put Indonesia out of their minds for Mei-mei's sake, so they could enjoy a special Chinese meal in the heart of New York's Chinatown.

Reading the *New York Times* newspaper in their hotel room that night, Naomi learned that a movie star had been at Ground Zero the day before. "Hey Mom! Too bad we missed her," she said to her mother.

"What else does it say?" Sara called from the bathroom, where she was bathing Mei-mei.

Naomi scanned the pages. After a few moments, her eyes rested on a headline on page three that made her gasp: *Riots in Indonesian Capital.* Naomi read the piece, and was dismayed to learn that Indonesians of Chinese descent again being targeted by crowds in several neigbourhoods in Jakarta. Naomi looked up to make sure that her mother was still in the bathroom with Mei-mei. Slowly, and silently, she folded the newspaper and placed it under her bed. *Mom's had enough bad news for one day,* Naomi thought to herself, *she doesn't need to know more about this.* Naomi thought for a moment of the Chinese families she knew in Lombok; several students who went to Kartini's School were of Chinese descent, Naomi knew, and she hoped that they were safe and not worried.

"Naomi, what else does the paper say?" Sara asked again.

Naomi went over to the bathroom with Mei-mei's pyjamas, and forced a smile. "It says that some great shows are playing on Broadway."

"Well, it's a good thing Dale got us some tickets for that show— whatever that show is—then," said Sara, as she lifted Mei-mei out of the bath and held her dripping body close. Naomi watched as water from Mei-mei's wet body darkened her mother's shirt. Mei-mei giggled, oblivious to the sombre mood.

Naomi could tell that her mother had become quite despondent, and she shared those feelings. They had three more days to explore New York, and Dale had left them with a long list of things to do and see; so much that they would hardly have time to think about anything else if they were to complete everything on it. But now, despite the excitement she had had about being in New York City, Naomi couldn't help but wonder what was happening back in Lombok. *Is everyone okay? Is everyone safe? Are you afraid?* Naomi wanted to get back to Indonesia and find out, but she knew there was more to her feelings than her concern for others' safety. New York was a dream come true, Naomi admitted, and it had not disappointed. Naomi was marvelling at the energy of the people, who gave the city its hum. And although Naomi and her mother both agreed that the towering steel-and-glass environment of Manhattan was impressive in its own way, Naomi knew that she was feeling a coldness that was not due just to the season. Naomi began to realize that she was missing the green forests and mountains of her island; the sea, and its endless shimmering. She was missing the smiles and warmth of all the people she was only just starting to know and love; Noor's family, and all her students, the hotel staff, the smiling old ladies in the markets of Senggigi and Mataram. She was homesick for Lombok.

"I'll dress Mei-mei," Naomi said. She reached to take the giggling girl and held her close despite the fact that she was still very wet, just as her mother had. Naomi turned and left the bathroom before her mother could see her tears. Naomi hugged her sister and wondered how Jameela and Fathima were doing. She wondered if their parents—and Steve—were worried, too. She thought of Noor, wondering how he was doing and if he was thinking of her.

17

NAOMI LOOKED OVER AT HER MOTHER, and saw that she was staring out the window. Her gaze shifted to the black oval behind her mother's profile; it was the middle of the night. Naomi felt a growing worry continue to gnaw away at her; she realized that her mother had been sitting that way for a good deal of the flight. She looked down at her sleeping sister and then turned her attention back to the in-flight movie. It was a comedy, but halfway into the movie Naomi realized with exasperation that she did not know what the story was about. She looked back at her mother, who was still staring out at the black night. Naomi leaned over to look at the channel indicator on her mother's armrest: her earphones were tuned to the movie soundtrack channel, but she had not been watching the show.

"Mom, are you all right?"

Sara started, and Naomi thought her mother's wide eyes showed more than a hint of alarm, quickly masked. Naomi wanted to believe that she had imagined it.

"You're not interested in the movie?"

"Oh…not really. I'm just tired from all the sightseeing."

Naomi nodded and turned back to face the movie screen on the seatback in front of her, and with increasing unease realized that despite the fatigue her mother spoke of, she hadn't been trying to fall asleep. They had been travelling for almost two days, and her mother had been uncharacteristically quiet for much of that time. Not even a chance to spend the night in Honolulu had brought out her usual excitement for the chance to explore a new place. Naomi knew her mother had done her best to appear enthusiastic, but she knew her mother—something was troubling her deeply.

The movie faded into a blur once again as Naomi thought back to their arrival in Honolulu the day before. When they had gotten to their hotel, Sara had immediately called Steve in Lombok. *I was putting on Mei-mei's bathing suit,* Naomi recalled. *I guess I wasn't paying too much attention to Mom. Mom wasn't talking. There was a lot to do. I had taken Mei-mei downstairs to buy sunblock—*

Naomi's skin prickled. She remembered that her mother had been in the washroom when she had returned from her errand. Her mother had taken a long time, but when she came out she was wearing her bathing suit, hat, and sunglasses. "I'm ready for the sun and the sand, after all that New York cold!" she had said, full of enthusiasm. At the time, Naomi had thought nothing of it, but now, looking back, Naomi realized her mother hadn't removed her sunglasses for quite a while afterwards; they had soon headed out to enjoy the beach. Naomi wondered if her mother had been hiding her eyes.

Something has happened. Steve told her something—and Mom isn't telling me. Naomi was sure of it. She turned to her mother again, ready to find out if her assumption was true, but Sara's eyes were closed. It would have to wait. Naomi looked down at her armrest and flipped through the channels, stopping when she heard the familiar sounds of the Balinese gamelan. The music had been oddly discordant to Naomi's ear at first, but soon it was all she wanted to listen to. She smiled, rested her hands in her lap and settled back in her seat. The melody, exotic and lyrical, soon began to lull Naomi, working its magic. *If I'm right,* she thought with a sigh...*I'll find out soon enough.*

•　　•　　•　　•　　•　　•

Naomi gasped when she stepped out of the airplane in Lombok. There were over thirty uniformed soldiers stationed around the airport, and two stood at the foot of the stairs to the plane. Naomi walked in nervous silence as she and the others passengers were led into the terminal building. "It wasn't like this when we left," she mumbled to her mother.

"I know, honey. Don't worry," her mother replied, looking back at her daughter. To Naomi, it looked as if her mother was ready to apologize for something. "Steve will explain."

Naomi found it hard to swallow. *It was true.* She walked in silence through the small airport, and almost collapsed with relief when she saw a smiling Steve in the arrivals hall as they passed through the immigration area. He stepped forward and scooped the three of them up in a big bear hug. Naomi kissed his cheek.

"What did things look like in Bali? Could you see anything from the airport?" asked Steve as he grabbed the luggage trolley. Naomi thought he seemed agitated.

"We had to stay on board. They wouldn't let us off the plane. But there's a lot of soldiers there, too," replied Sara. "It looks more...noticeable here. This airport's a lot smaller."

Steve's smile had started to fade. Sara and Steve exchanged glances. Naomi noticed that he was moving quickly. As they neared the doors, Naomi could see that Steve's jeep was parked on the street, and Wahab was at the wheel. "Get in," Steve said. He threw the luggage in the back of the vehicle. Sara gently pulled Naomi and Mei-mei ahead of her into the back seat. Wahab sped away as soon as the doors were shut, and they made their way towards Mataram.

Naomi looked around with a growing anxiety. Green military vehicles seemed to be everywhere on the streets. Traffic was light; there were only a few trucks and cars and taxis. But something else was not right. The air was warm and humid; always a jolt after any time in colder climates, but Naomi didn't notice. She shivered; it was early evening, the time of day in Lombok when people took to the streets after a day of work. But now, Naomi's eyes searched the streets and sidewalks frantically for signs of life.

"Mom?" she cried out in a trembling voice.

"Naomi—" Steve began.

"Steve? What's happening?"

"There's been rioting today in Mataram. Some looting..." he began. He sighed, then turned in the seat to face Naomi and her mother. "It's...under control...for the time being—"

"Wahab, what do you think is going to happen?" Sara asked.

Naomi looked at Wahab's hands firmly clenching the steering wheel. "I think... history is going to repeat itself in Indonesia."

"It's pretty tense..."

Naomi looked at Steve, not believing what he was saying. She turned to her mother and saw that she was crying. Naomi felt like she couldn't breathe.

"Tourists are leaving…and there was an evacuation of foreign personnel today. At least fifty expatriate families. They were lined up at the airport for hours. I didn't know there were no many of us here—"

"Steve!" Naomi heard her mother gasp.

"Don't worry. Wahab and I are working on it."

"What are you saying?" questioned Sara. Naomi could hear the fear in her voice. "Are you really concerned about this—"

"In the past, there have been riots in other parts on the country, as you know. But not in Lombok…not until now—" said Wahab.

"Wahab—your family!" Sara suddenly cried out. "How are Farah and the kids?"

"They are at home. Safe."

Naomi was taking the information in, trying to process it. She sat back in her seat, and looked out the window. Lombok was as beautiful as it was when she had left for New York City. *How could this place have become dangerous?* Her thoughts turned to Bali; to her and millions of people around the world, it had also been a haven of peace and beauty and tranquility. All of a sudden Naomi felt tired. She looked over at Mei-mei on the seat beside her and wished that she, too, could put all this out of her head.

They were now passing through central Mataram. Naomi looked around, wondering if she was where she thought she was. Things looked so different without people. A few shops had been boarded up. A makeshift barricade, made of planks of wood, had been erected in front of the bank.

"Someone threw a cinder block into the window at the bank. The rupiah nosedived again," Steve said.

"Again?" Sara asked, "How much this time?"

"Not worth much now—"

"Dear God."

"Good thing Steve gets paid in US dollars," Wahab said. Naomi was surprised to hear this joke again. But this time she felt sick; it had become a cruel joke. Wahab chuckled feebly. Naomi saw Steve turn to his friend, and rest his hand on Wahab's shoulder.

Suddenly Naomi found herself thinking of the girl she had seen talking on the phone in the hotel business centre, when she had gone there for the first time—the young Canadian who had been teaching English in Jakarta. *It was only a few months ago, but now everything has changed,* Naomi thought to herself. *Maybe she left long ago, looking for a place that might be safer. Maybe Japan.* Naomi remembered that Thailand was also popular with young graduates as a nice place to live and teach English—and then reminded herself that there was speculation that Muslim extremists would strike there next.

"How's the school?" Naomi asked.

Wahab spoke up. "There's no problem with the school. No one has touched it. Farah is eager to get the new term underway...well, I don't know what's going to happen now—"

"That sounds like good news," interrupted Sara. Naomi looked over to see her mother smiling wanly. "We need to think about training more teachers. Or even hiring...perhaps hiring some Canadian students, or other English-speaking foreigners..." she stopped as if in mid-thought. Naomi was surprised by her mother's comments. *Don't you realize what Wahab is saying, Mom?* With a sick feeling, Naomi wondered if the school would ever open for business again. She thought of her students, and of her own pride, and her mother's and Farah's pride, at being the owners and teachers of Kartini's School.

I wonder how Noor is doing, Naomi thought. She regretted not sending him a postcard. She wondered if he had missed her, and if he had thought about her. She wondered what he was doing at that moment; she had often thought about him—and admitted this to herself. She wanted to see him, and felt excited that she was going to see him soon; she would call him tomorrow.

Wahab was turning into the gravel drive of Naomi's home. Farah and the twins were standing in front of the house. Jameela and Fathima were smiling brightly and jumping with excitement. Noor was standing next to them, looking down at his sisters and Naomi knew what he was thinking. She smiled. He looked up and looked right at Naomi as the Jeep came to a stop in the driveway. A smile flickered on his face as he moved forward to open the door for Naomi. Suddenly Naomi felt nervous. She stepped out of the Jeep and went straight to the twins who were crowding around Mei-mei and Sara. Wahab's wife reached over to give Sara and Naomi warm hugs.

"Welcome back. We missed you. We all missed you," she said, looking over at Noor, who stood silently, and somewhat awkwardly, off to the side. He looked at everyone and said. "Yeah, we all missed you." Naomi felt his eyes rest on her, and she felt nervous and happy once again.

"We had a fabulous time, and we'll tell you all about it," Sara replied. "But we are all so glad to be back. New York City is amazing, but I think I'm an island girl now." She laughed. "I am ready to get back to my Lombok life." Naomi knew the exchange was for the benefit of the little girls in the group. There was an awkward silence.

"And we're so glad to get you all back with us," beamed Farah.

Wahab and Steve began to unload the vehicle and everyone took a piece of luggage, even the twins, and carried them to the house. Naomi looked over at her mother and saw that she was huddled in the kitchen with Farah; both had sombre expressions. Naomi knew that Farah would be filling Sara in on the rioting that had happened earlier that day in Mataram. Naomi watched the women, and it reminded her of New York, watching her mother and Dale discussing something very similar. In an instant, Naomi's feelings of happiness and relief at being home in Lombok had been exchanged for feelings of sadness, almost despair. Naomi sighed, and hefted her carry-on bag down the hall. She looked around and found Mei-mei with the twins in her bedroom. Mei-mei had thrown open her own bag and was showing Jameela and Fathima the two giant lollipops that Dale had bought for her at a special candy shop on 52nd Street. Naomi's breath caught as Mei-mei handed them over to the twins, who looked at each other and then to Mei-mei and said "thank you" with big hugs.

"We're so glad to be back. I want to go sit on our beach. How about you Mei-mei?" asked Naomi, as she walked into her sister's room.

Mei-mei's eyes lit up. "Yes, Naomi! C'mon Jameela Fathima. Let's go!" Mei-mei was hurriedly undressing and making her way to her dresser at the same time, she pulled out some shorts and a T-shirt. Naomi and the twins burst out laughing.

"Yes, let's go," Naomi said. The twins nodded. Naomi went to her room, peeled off her airplane clothes, and slipped on some jeans and her favourite tunic, the batik one that the twins had given her at Christmas. It felt good to put it on.

Jameela took Mei-mei's hand and Fathima and Naomi followed behind them to the beach. On their way Naomi called out to the others where they were going. Even though she had wanted to see Noor, now that she was back she just didn't know what to do about it. She didn't know what to say to him, and she was glad to be out of the house. Naomi breathed deeply, letting the air fill her head with smells and her heart with peace, as it always did, but this time, the peace in her heart was not complete, and her mind was not cleared of the growing fear and uncertainty of the recent events. Naomi looked over at the twins as they walked along the beach, and wondered how much they knew. *They must know something*, Naomi decided. *After all, they're not kids. They can figure things out for themselves. If their parents haven't told them, they would have been able to find out from others about what had happened today in Mataram.*

But if they were afraid, Jameela and Fathima were not showing it now, not to Mei-mei. The three young girls were already seated in the sand, facing the island of Bali, and their feet were already covered in sand washed in on the waves. They giggled as the waves rode past them, getting their bottoms and hands wet as well. *Not a care in the world…*Naomi thought. *Or maybe they are just being brave.* Naomi sat down in the sand, farther back on the beach closer to the trees, and watched them play. The sun was setting, like fire in the sky, behind Gunung Agung. Naomi stared into the sky, and began making plans. She couldn't help it; it was irresistible. She didn't want to leave. *I'll go into Senggigi tomorrow and get the school ready, I'll go to the hotel and check my email. Maybe what happened in Mataram didn't even make the news overseas. I want to re-open the school as soon as possible—*

"So, how was your trip?"

Naomi looked up, then sat up straight. Noor sat down in the sand next to her. He as smiling at her and Naomi felt she could hardly breathe. "I wonder if you're glad to be back, after having the chance to go to New York City. What do you call it? The Big Apple?" Noor asked. Naomi nodded, forcing herself to smile, and to look natural.

Why does Noor always make me feel so…so… Naomi couldn't figure it out. Sometimes, he angered her. Sometimes he made her nervous. But sometimes he made her feel a way she had never felt before.

"Why do they call it that, anyway?

Naomi had to smile at Noor's query. "I have no idea," she replied. "But it is big." Noor smiled. "We're glad to be back." There was a pause, and both Noor and Naomi turned to look at their siblings playing together. "We went to Ground Zero," Naomi said after a while.

Noor's eyebrows shot up, "Wow." That was all, and then, "We have our own Ground Zero here—"

"I know. I heard," Naomi replied in a whisper. "Your dad and Steve told us on the way here."

"The new shopping mall in Mataram has been destroyed. Burnt out. There was even some damage and vandalism in the marketplace. But it is still open for business. People have pitched tents. They're still selling."

"They're very brave," replied Naomi, then wondered if *desperate* was the better word. If there was no trade these people would have no income at all, Naomi knew. Suddenly Naomi felt tired. *Why do people have to suffer—people who didn't do anything to anyone?* "I hope nothing else happens."

"Me, too," replied Noor. "But…I'm afraid…"

Naomi looked over at Noor. "Don't be afr—"

"No, I'm not afraid. I just…know…something is going to happen."

18

delapan belas

"WHAT ARE YOU TALKING ABOUT?" Naomi whispered.

Noor took Naomi's hand. "I know something is going to happen here, again. The students at the university are planning a demonstration. A big one. Farmers, too, from the area where the government wants to put that airport." Noor took a breath. "I thought after what happened in Jakarta that the students and the farmers would cancel it...*but they're not going to.*"

Naomi could feel the hair stand up at the back of her neck. "Noor! Tell Wahab! Tell your dad. He'll do something. He'll sort it out."

"No. It could be dangerous for him to get involved now...there are certain people who already know what is going to happen. They'll be waiting."

"Are you involved?"

"There are some things you need to know," Noor began. Naomi couldn't breathe. "What happened today was only the beginning. I know it. My father and Steve know it, too. You have to leave. There are no more foreigners left, only a few journalists waiting for some action. Things have already started to get out of control."

"What about—"

"Our dads are working on a plan," Noor said. He put his hands on Naomi's shoulders.

"Wait...How do you know?" demanded Naomi. She didn't want to believe what he was telling her. She wondered how Noor could be so sure of what was going to happen.

"*I know,*" replied Noor impatiently. "I told you. There is going to be more rioting—and it won't just be angry town people looting the Chinese shops or the shopping mall. My friends at the university told me about the demonstration near Mataram. The farmers are going to protest. Their land is going to be taken from them. They don't feel they have any choice." Naomi could feel Noor's grip tighten. "It could be thousands. And right now, I know, the government will not let that happen. It's the last thing they want right now…It could mean big trouble…even right here in Senggigi."

"What are you saying?"

"You saw all the military vehicles. They are waiting," whispered Noor. "They know what is going to happen. They are ready—"

Naomi's eyes widened.

"—and when it happens…then, I think—this time—everyone will run amok."

Naomi stared at Noor. Her heart was pounding in her chest. "What can we do?"

Noor began to reply, but Jameela and Fathima and Mei-mei came running up to them, out of breath. "Can we go home now?" Mei-mei asked her sister.

Noor picked up the little girl and gave her a kiss. "Good idea, Mei-mei. It's bedtime," he said. He passed Mei-mei over to Naomi and continued. "Take your sister and go home and…listen to Steve. Be ready."

They walked back to the house, just as their parents were heading their way to get them. "Ah, our children," said Wahab, "What a lovely sight to see." Naomi could hear the fatigue in his voice. She wondered what they had been discussing inside the house.

Farah put her arm around Naomi's shoulders. Naomi could feel a slight quaking, a trembling, and Naomi wondered if it was Farah's or her own. Not much was said as Noor and his family departed, only good-bye, spoken as if they would meet again tomorrow, as usual.

Mei-mei was given her bath before bedtime, and Naomi went to her bedroom and shut the door. She didn't know what to say to her parents; she wasn't even sure if Noor knew what he was talking about. Naomi flopped down onto her bed and stared at the ceiling, listening to Mei-mei's giggles from down the corridor. Naomi looked around her room, and her eyes rested on the pile of teaching materials in the corner. A lump came to her throat and tears stung her eyes. Kartini's School was closed, and Naomi knew that it would never reopen. They had only just begun.

Naomi felt afraid, she felt afraid for everyone in Senggigi. She thought about the people who had started the rioting in Mataram, and the victims, not understanding why it had to be.

Naomi sat down by the pile of books and papers, and reached for a thick file. She opened it, looking at the writing and pictures of her youngest students, and their names spelled neatly at the bottom corners of the pages. These works of art were from a lesson about Christmas. The children had enjoyed drawing pictures of Santa and brightly coloured Christmas trees, decorated with pictures of snowmen, angels, bells, and candles. Naomi almost smiled as she remembered the party they had organized. The students had decorated a tree. Steve had come to be the Santa, and Naomi had been surprised at what a great Santa he had been. Some of the parents, mostly mothers, had come to hear their children sing Christmas songs. Naomi had worked hard on the Christmas show; it had been a busy, exhilarating time. The children had learned about Christmas, but even better, Naomi thought, she had learned so much from them. Naomi remembered cleaning up after the party was over; Farah had been humming a Christmas carol. She had turned to Naomi to say, 'We'll do a Valentine's Day party, then we have to get to work on play about Kartini, to celebrate Kartini Day.' *I really wanted to write a play with Farah about Kartini,* Naomi thought bitterly.

She looked at the painting in her lap. It was of a Christmas tree, beautifully and colourfully rendered. The decorations; drums, bells, candles, and snowmen, were labelled neatly in English. Naomi looked at the words, whispering their meanings in *bahasa: gendang, lonceng, lilin.* Naomi smiled as she stared at the word *snowman.* She had been surprised when her students told her there was no word for it in their language. And then she had laughed with delight, as well as pride, when a boy named Ihsan explained in broken English that there was no snow on Lombok. The class then made up their own name for snowman: orangsneeuw. *Orang* means "human"; and *sneeuw* is the Dutch word for "snow." They had had a wonderful time inventing the word.

There would be no more students, no more school. No more smiles and laughter. No more learning together. No more proud parents and students and teachers.

Naomi leaned back against the bookshelf and looked at the clock. It was past midnight now, but she wasn't tired. She heard the faint sound of her parents talking in the kitchen. Naomi got up and walked down the hall, she stopped short and held her breath.

"We're getting out of here," Naomi heard Steve whispering. "I've contacted Mike. He's going to get us out."

"What? Is this…like a secret, or something?"

"Yes, Sara. We have to do this quietly. It won't work any other way. We screwed up. Nobody can help us now. That flight to Sydney was the last chance and we lost it."

"What do you mean nobody is going to help us?"

"Sara, look, we've got to do this on our own. I got hold of Mike, he's coming to get us. We can't tell anyone—"

"Steve? What about Farah and Wahab and the kids? Aren't they—aren't we all— in the same danger—"

"Of course, they're coming with us. But that's all. Mike was clear on that. It can't get out of hand. Or else the whole thing will fall apart."

Naomi could hear her mother's anguish. "I see…I know."

Naomi stood frozen as she listened to her parents' conversation. She didn't want to believe what Steve was saying. But she knew. Steve was talking about an escape.

"Day after tomorrow. We'll get ourselves to the airport by the site. Not the domestic airport, the construction site—"

"But there's not even a runway there," Sara whispered.

"No, it's a field. Mike says he can manage it. He's done it before."

"How are we going to get there…if there's trouble?"

"We'll leave in the middle of the night, wait for dawn." There was a pause. "We'll have to leave everything behind. Steve reached forward and hugged Sara. I'm sorry that it has come to this. I'm so sorry that we didn't sort this out when you were in Hawaii. I just didn't want to believe it—"

"That was my doing. I didn't want to believe it, either," replied Sara. "I see now how foolish I was. I could have taken the girls to Canada. I just…had no idea—"

Naomi stepped into the room. "What…are you talking about?"

Sara and Steve looked up. "Honey. We've got to get out of here —"

Naomi looked angrily from one to another. "So we're running away like frightened rabbits? We're escaping? Steve, why aren't you doing something?" Naomi cried out, surprising even herself. "You work for the UN! Don't you have any power? Do something! Can't you do…*something*? Don't just try to run away—"

"Naomi!" said Sara gently.

"You're a coward!"

"Now you've said enough, Naomi!" Sara spoke sharply. Her voice was quavering, but Naomi knew it was with anger more than anything else. "Whay are you talking like that to your father?"

"It's okay, Sara," replied Steve quietly, as he reached for Sara's hand. "Naomi's under a lot of stress right now…we all are. He looked over at Naomi, and she instantly felt ashamed. It wasn't what she really felt. She felt like a coward herself.

"Dad—"

"Naomi…" Steve interrupted. He looked for a long time at Naomi and appeared to be wanting to say something, or was perhaps thinking of something to say. Then it looked as if he changed his mind. His shoulders fell. "Please, Naomi. Just trust me on this. Just trust me."

"Go to bed, Naomi," Sara said. Naomi could hear the coldness in her mother's voice. "We'll talk in the morning."

Naomi did not reply. She turned and walked back towards her bedroom. Her cheeks burned, her stomach was clenched in a knot. She felt angry and embarrassed and ashamed. But she was also afraid. She had been afraid for a long time. Naomi stopped at Mei-mei's bedroom door and looked in. For a moment she let herself be carried away by the sound of her little sister's peaceful breathing. Naomi wanted to cry. Naomi crept inside her sister's room, watched her sister sleeping in the darkness, then slipped into bed beside her. She was glad to be in the darkness, glad to be alone with her sister who seemed to be oblivious to all that was happening around them—for the moment, at least.

Naomi reached out to hold Mei-mei's hand, listened to her breathing, and could feel her own heart pounding in her chest. Naomi recalled her parents' conversation. After a while, Naomi thought she could understand why her parents were planning their escape. Naomi knew that some of the victims of the riot in Mataram were not only tourists, but Indonesian business owners, some of whom were of Chinese descent. *Maybe Mom is worried about you, Mei-mei. They want to protect you…they want to protect me, too.* Naomi knew this was the truth, but she couldn't help feel ashamed. *We're going to run away, but who's going to protect everyone else? We need to be here to help. There must be something we can do,* Naomi wondered, then admitted to herself that she couldn't think of the answer.

What will happen to Wahab's family? What will happen to Noor? We will be leaving together, Steve said. But where are they going to end up? Maybe Mom and Steve and I will end up in Canada, or maybe England. But what about Noor and his family? Especially Noor. He wouldn't want to be anywhere but here. Naomi thought sadly. Naomi wiped tears from her face. *What's going to happen next?*

Naomi lay all night in bed next to Mei-mei, unable to sleep. And when the morning call from the neighbourhood mosque began at 4:30, Naomi began to pray.

19

NAOMI HEARD THE SOUND of a vehicle drive up to the house, then the sound of the front door open and close. It was still dark outside. Naomi was frightened. She got up and opened the bedroom door, and was shocked to see Farah, Fathima, and Jameela crossing into the living room.

"What's happening?" Naomi said as she entered the room. Wahab and Steve were huddled together, talking quietly. Sara emerged from her bedroom with a small dufflebag in her hand. She looked at Naomi, and Naomi could see that her mother's eyes were swollen. Without a word, Sara crossed the hall into Mei-mei's room.

"It is beginning," Wahab said.

Steve came over, and put his hands on Naomi's shoulders. "Change of plans. We're leaving now. Get some things. One bag."

Naomi's mouth felt dry. Her heart was racing and her arms felt weak. Naomi returned to her bedroom and grabbed a duffle from under her bed. She threw in her book bag with her wallet in it. From the top of her dresser, Naomi grabbed the photo of herself with her students, and some photos of the trip to Mount Rinjani, and threw them into the bag, too. She pulled out some jeans and a T-shirt and put them on without a thought. She looked around her room, and her eyes rested on the pile of papers that she had been looking at the day before. She grabbed the papers, her students' work, and stuffed them into the duffle. Tears were running down her cheeks now, dripping onto the crumpled pages. Naomi was breathing hard. She looked in her closet, yanked a batik shirt off a hanger and put it on over her T-shirt, threw another one into the bag, then grabbed her bag and left the room. The others were already filing out the front door.

Naomi could hear a vehicle coming down the road from the north, on its way to Senggigi. Trembling, she walked to the end of the drive to see what it was. A half-ton truck was heading towards her, and Naomi could see that the back was filled with men, standing and holding what appeared to be unfurled banners, as well as large sticks of bamboo. Naomi was frozen. The vehicle slowed down as it passed her. The driver shouted at her in *bahasa* and motioned for her to go back, back into the house. Naomi looked up at the men as the vehicle passed. Some looked down at her, their eyes staring. From their gestures, some seemed to be reiterating what the driver had said, but Naomi did not know what it was for sure. Naomi saw words written on plywood boards along the sides of the truck: *SIAP REVOLUSI!* and FARMERS STAY! WIRANO OUT!

Naomi felt a hand on her arm and whirled around. It was Wahab.

"Come, Naomi—"

"Wahab? What's going to happen?" Naomi choked back a sob.

"We have run amok," said Wahab sadly. "They are targeting the churches, the Chinese businesses, the hotels. We saw it already on our way here—"

"Who?" asked Naomi. "The farmers?"

Wahab gave Naomi a gentle hug. "No. The farmers have a right to be angry," Wahab replied, then shook his head. "But they will pay dearly for daring to defy the government. As for the others, they are the same people who rioted in Mataram. And Jakarta. They are not finished." Wahab put his hands on Naomi's shoulders. "Naomi, sometimes, when people feel they have nothing left, they do things they would not normally do. When people react as a group, they lose their sense of identity; their sense of right and wrong. That is what happened yesterday in Mataram. It happened in Jakarta. In Borneo, before. And, I fear, it is going to continue today in Senggigi. We must hurry—"

"Where's Noor?" Naomi asked, trying hard to keep her rising panic at bay.

"I told him to take Mike to the plane. He'll be there, waiting," Wahab replied. Naomi clutched Wahab's arm as she walked with him. She thought she might faint.

At the steps to the house, Naomi picked up her bag and opened the door to Steve's Jeep. "We're going to take my car, Naomi," said Wahab, forcing a smile. "I am sorry it is not a more luxurious model."

Everyone piled into Wahab's car. Fathima sat on Naomi's lap. Jameela was seated next to her, on her mother's lap. Sara held Mei-mei. No one spoke. Naomi looked at her house for the last time, and was surprised to see the curtains opening behind the large living-room window. Then she saw Steve through the window. She watched, bewildered, as he placed a large potted plant on the table, right in the centre of the window. Moments later he emerged from the house. He did not lock the front door. Wahab was already in the driver's seat, with the motor running. As soon as Steve got in the car, Wahab backed out of the drive and headed towards Senggigi.

Steve turned to everyone in the back seat. "Okay, we're heading to the field where Mike and Noor are waiting for us. It is not the airport, it is a place in the interior, but we have to pass through Senggigi and make our way to the northern part of Mataram before we get to the road we need to take." To Naomi, it looked like Steve was going to say more, but instead, he pursed his lips and nodded to Sara, then turned to the front. Naomi couldn't see her mother's face in the crowded back seat.

Within minutes they were entering the town of Senggigi. Naomi could see armoured vehicles in the road, and soldiers with their rifles hoisted standing in front of the gate of the resort hotel that Naomi often went to. Naomi was horrified to see a plume of black smoke rising up from behind the thick hedge that bounded the grounds of the large resort. Faces entered Naomi's mind; smiling faces of her friends, the hotel staff. *Are they safe? If there are any tourists left, are they safe?* Fear gripped Naomi; she was afraid of what they would find farther down the road.

Through the car window she thought she could hear some shouting. There were people running across the main street, a hundred metres in front of their car. Wahab slowed down.

"My God. They're looting," said Sara.

Naomi craned her neck to see around Wahab. She saw two small boys carrying a large box on their shoulders. There was a picture of a television on the box. The boys were trying to run. Naomi swallowed hard. *They look so afraid.* She could see a soldier screaming at them from just a few yards away, waving them away with his free arm, while in his other arm he held his rifle high in the air. People were running in every direction. Naomi's eyes turned to the row of shops. The window of an electronics shop had been shattered, and a young man was emerging from it, stepping through the jagged glass. As their car passed, the young man looked at Naomi. In each hand he was holding an iPod. He raised them in triumph and grinned. Naomi struggled to make sense of what she was seeing. She couldn't cry; it was too confusing. Then she felt a rumble.

"We've got to move," Wahab said. Naomi turned to look over her shoulder, and saw another large armoured vehicle turn the corner from a side street behind them. Wahab began to honk his horn and Naomi felt the car accelerate slightly.

"Look at the church."

"The school! Look what they've done." Farah cried out.

"It is only a building, my love," said Wahab.

"No…It's not," said Farah. She bent her head and began to cry.

"Please, Farah—" said Sara.

"It's okay, Mama. Everything will be okay," said Jameela, in her mother's lap.

"We are Sasak, Mama. They will not hurt us," added Fathima. Naomi's stomach lurched; the girl sounded so afraid.

Farah looked up as Fathima spoke. Naomi could see the look of shock on Farah's face and then watched, helpless, as Farah's face crumpled into fresh, silent sobs.

"If that was Senggigi, I don't want to be in Mataram," mumbled Steve. "Is there another road we can take, Wahab?"

Wahab shook his head.

They continued south, towards Mataram. At one point, the road hugged the coastline, and Naomi looked across at the sea. There was Bali in the distance; the profile of Gunung Agung. Naomi stared at it, imprinting its image in her mind. She felt she would never see it again.

"Looks like a roadblock," muttered Wahab.

Naomi held her breath. Wahab brought the car to a stop in front of three men in military uniform. Wahab and the soldiers spoke to each other rapidly. It sounded to Naomi like a heated discussion. Naomi could tell Wahab was nervous, and she thought she kept hearing the word *tourist* over and over again. From her seat behind Wahab, Naomi could tell that Wahab was pointing to her in the back seat. One of the officers bent down to peer at her and the others seated beside her. Naomi saw Wahab lay his hands on the car window railing, imploring the men in uniform. Suddenly one of them, the senior officer, Naomi guessed, waved them through impatiently. Wahab's head was bowed as he thanked the men with guns. He put the car into gear and drove onwards to Mataram. The streets looked deserted.

"That was lucky," said Wahab when they had driven a little farther. The military have cordoned off Mataram. I fear the worst. I can feel it. We were lucky to get through. Our road is just ahead." Within moments, Wahab turned left, onto a narrow road. "We'll be there soon."

"Wahab," said Naomi after a while. "Where do you suppose those farmers and supporters went?"

Wahab let out a breath. Naomi could see him shaking his head. "I honestly don't know. May Allah protect them."

Ten minutes later, Naomi could see a small aircraft sitting at the edge of a field. Nearby, there were three small, prefab buildings inside a fenced-in area. A thick row of bushes and low palms lined one side; on the far side of the field, Naomi looked out at a fertile valley of rice fields, slightly terraced, rich and green. It was a beautiful valley, and Naomi wondered why no one had ever brought her to see it before.

"What is this place?" asked Sara.

"It's a...compound. It's not supposed to be here, actually," replied Steve. "This is where they are going to build that airport."

Naomi froze. "Where's Noor?" Her voice was shaking.

"He must be in the plane already, with Mike," replied Farah.

They got out of the car and started walking to the plane. Naomi could see Mike step out and wave.

Naomi began to run to Mike. She was out of breath when she reached him. "Where's Noor?"

"He's not with you?"

Naomi's voice cracked. "No!"

"Bloody hell."

Naomi heard a vehicle behind her, and she whirled around. A dark Jeep drove up and stopped next to Wahab's car. Naomi was surprised to see a blond couple emerge. Steve stopped and waited for them to catch up.

"This is Benny and Lucia. Steve said simply. "They're coming with us. They missed the boat, I guess—just like we did." Sara managed a smile and took the frightened woman's hand in her own.

"Nice day for a freedom flight," Mike said. Some in the forlorn group tried to smile back at Mike, knowing he was just trying to help cheer up the younger ones, but for Naomi, it was an unfortunate choice of words. They reminded her of what she and the others were doing; something so many people could not do. *We're not trying to help—we're running away.* Again, a feeling of shame washed over Naomi, along with her fear and nervousness.

"Okay, get in," Mike said. He led Sara and Mei-mei to the plane and stood by the stairs as Sara helped her little daughter climb the steps. Farah, Jameela and Fathima followed, and Naomi was behind them. Naomi took a seat by the window behind the pilot's seat.

"Where's Noor?" asked Farah. Naomi turned to look at her. Sara reached to hold Farah's hand, squeezing it tightly. Naomi turned away, unable to bear the frantic look in the woman's eyes.

Naomi peered through her window, looking for Steve and Wahab. She noticed that they were at the side of the plane, huddled together with Mike, talking intently. Naomi wondered what they were saying.

Where's Noor?

Mike opened the door to the cockpit and climbed in. He turned around. "Okay, buckle up."

"Wait!" cried Farah, her voice quavering. "Where's Noor!" she was beginning to panic.

Naomi thought she heard a noise. She looked out the window, in the direction of the small compound. A pick-up truck came careening around the corner, stopping behind the other vehicles. To Naomi's horror, she saw people jumping off the back of the pick-up truck and start racing towards the plane. *They're going to kill us!*

"Wahab! Steve! What's going on?" Mike shouted out above the sound of the engines. Naomi watched as Steve and Wahab began running away from the plane, towards the group of people that had just arrived. As the group got closer, Naomi could see things more clearly. The people running to the plane were not thugs, or the police. There were women and children. Naomi watched as Wahab grabbed a child under each arm and began running with the crowd back towards the plane. Another truck drove up and more women and children began their dash. Naomi saw Steve stop. He looked at the plane, then he turned back to the newest arrivals.

Noor!

Noor was helping an elderly woman. Then he reached behind him to grab a young child who had stopped and was starting to cry.

Naomi couldn't breathe. She watched the scene unfold in front of her, trying to make sense of what was happening. The people were beginning to climb into the plane, some were smiling, some were crying. Naomi saw that her mother had removed her seatbelt and was trying to help some mothers and children fasten their own belts. One woman refused to let go of her daughter who was clinging to her in her lap. The plane was filling up quickly.

Naomi turned back to the window. Steve was coming with the group of stragglers. A woman was carrying a child on her back. Wahab had run back to help.

Who are these people?

Naomi stared at Noor. He was now carrying a child on his back. The old woman and some other children were following him. They were dressed in worn clothes. Naomi had never seen them before.

"Bloody hell!" cried Mike. He started to get out of the cockpit, but Wahab waved him back in. He was shouting, but Naomi could hear none of it. Naomi watched as the last of the group of stragglers continued their dash to the plane. Suddenly, they all ducked at the same moment. Naomi saw them look away suddenly, in the same direction, and she was momentarily surprised. Then she felt sick.

"Shit!" Naomi could hear Mike shout above the sound of the engines and the noise in the plane. "Dammit!"

"Steve!" Sara shouted.

"Wahab! Noor!" cried Farah. Naomi could hear Mei-mei and Jamilla and Fathima crying.

There was a commotion behind her as some people made their way into the now-crowded plane, lying in the aisles, on each other's laps, but Naomi barely noticed. There were people still running towards the plane, and Naomi could almost hear their shouts of fear and confusion. Some ran to the plane, but then a small group had begun running for cover in the opposite direction. The group had splintered. Steve ran to Mike's door and threw a small child in his lap.

"Wahab! Jesus Christ! Steve?"

Steve waved him off. Then he turned and looked directly at Naomi through the window. It was as if, to Naomi, time was standing still now. She watched Steve begin to raise his arm as he looked at her, and then he turned and ran with Wahab and Noor back in the direction of the trees, where some of the crowd had fled, and others, mostly women and children, were still heading. Naomi had never felt so helpless and afraid, as she watched their retreating figures. She saw Steve stop and turn, for the last time, shouting at Mike and motioning for him to get going.

"Bloody hell!" Mike shouted. He looked at the boy in his lap. "Take him, Naomi. Switch places if there's no more room back there." He threw the small boy over to Naomi then slammed his door shut. Naomi buckled the boy in her seat, then clambered over into the seat next to Mike, and watched, petrified, as he prepared for take-off, wishing that everything were all just a nightmare. The engines began to rev. Naomi could see the propellers start to move. She began to hyperventilate.

"STEVE!" Sara wailed.

"Daddy!" Naomi heard Mei-mei cry out in her small voice. Naomi could hear screams behind her. She could hear her mother crying. She thought she could hear Farah talking to her daughters. Naomi couldn't speak. She could only watch, helplessly, as Mike applied full throttle, and the plane accelerated across the field.

There were shouts and anguished cries from some of the people in the back of the plane. Both her mother and Farah were now silent. Naomi was surprised to hear weak cheers from a few of the children as the plane let go of the land and began to rise. Some were too young to know what was happening around them, but Mei-mei knew that something was dreadfully wrong. Naomi heard some weeping nearby and she turned around. The boy she had traded places with was sitting by himself, crying.

Naomi wondered if any of his family were on the plane and with a sinking feeling she realized that there was a good chance he was all alone now; Naomi remembered seeing a woman and two other children rush into the trees ahead of Noor and Wahab when the chaos had begun. She looked at the weeping boy and turned away, sick with fear for him—and for all of them.

What's happening out there?

Naomi looked out the window as the plane rose into the sky. She couldn't see anyone now. After several minutes, Steve circled and flew back over the field. Naomi saw several armoured vehicles sitting at one end of the field now. She saw several more, smaller vehicles approaching the field from another road. Naomi thought she was going to be sick; she could clearly see two bodies lying on the ground in front of one of the vehicles. She looked at the motionless bodies, not believing what is was she was seeing, hoping that if she looked at them long enough they would turn out to be something other than what she knew they were. She hoped that if she looked long enough, she would see Steve and Noor and Wahab come running out of the trees. And they would look up at the plane and wave and smile. *This can't be happening*—

Naomi reached for some headphones in front of her and put them on. Mike looked over at Naomi, and she saw that he had been crying. Reflexively, Naomi began to wipe tears from her face; she didn't know she had been crying, too.

"Naomi, when the time comes, I need you to help me. This plane is overloaded, but we're going to make it out of here in one piece—"

"Where are we going?" Naomi asked, surprising herself by asking the question.

"The plan was to get to Darwin," Mike replied. "But we can't make it that far. We'll have to see how far we can get. I've got a couple cans of fuel in the back, but we'll still have to land this thing—"

"Okay," Naomi replied softly. "Okay."

"We're going to make it," Naomi heard Mike's voice through the headphones. "We are all going to make it—because that's what they want us to do." Naomi looked at Mike as he spoke. He was checking the gauges. She saw on his face an expression of determination, and concentration. He looked over at Naomi, "You'll get through this, Naomi. No matter what happens," he said. "Trust me, you will."

Naomi nodded, just beginning to comprehend what Mike was saying to her. She was grateful that the headphones could muffle the sounds of the women and children who were crying in the back of the plane.

20

To love someone deeply gives you strength.
Being loved by someone deeply gives you courage.
– Lao-Tzu

THE DOORBELL RANG, AND NAOMI got up from her small desk.

"Hello…Naomi? Nice to meet you, finally. I'm Donna, the Columbia University journalism student Dale told you about…Thanks for letting me interview you for my article on third culture kids. Although I can see you're not a kid any more." The woman smiled.

Naomi smiled back. "Well, I've been living apart from my mother since, well, almost four years now. I guess that makes me not a kid any more."

"Still on the move, though?" Donna asked, as she lifted her large wool poncho over her head and looked around for a place to put it.

"Off and on. Mostly field sessions while I was earning my degree. Spent a summer in Tanzania…I'll just put that on the chair over here. "

"Great…thanks…Wow, Tanzania."

"Hope you don't mind sitting on my bed. As you can see, we don't have much room in this cramped apartment, even though I am living the New York Dream."

Donna giggled again. "Yeah, you've got the dream. Young intern for the United Nations. Going to make your mark on the world all right. She laughed to herself as she fished her tape recorder out of her big bag. "Don't mind if I use one of these?" Donna placed the small device on the table between them.

"Go ahead."

"Too bad you're not a movie star. You could be a UN goodwill ambassador. That's so much more glamourous than doing what you do...uh...what do you do?"

"I work at the liaison office of the United Nations Settlements Program. My roommate, Worokia, works for he United Nations High Commission for Refugees."

"Right. Sounds boring, if I do say so. Not like UNICEF. Everyone knows them. How does one end up working in the liaison office of the United Nations.... Never mind, I'm getting ahead of myself. Okay, let's start at the beginning. Tell me where you were born and how you became a third-culture kid."

"Okay," replied Naomi, stifling a sigh. "I was born in Portage la Prairie, Manitoba. When I was 12, my mother and I moved to northern Japan, where we lived for a year. After returning to Manitoba for a year, we decided we liked being explorers, we liked living that kind of life—and so my mother got a job in Hong Kong. We lived there for just over two years. During that time, my mother married a man from Yorkshire, England. Later, he—Steve—got a job working on a UN-sponsored project on the island of Lombok, in Indonesia."

"Lombok. Spell that please."

"L-o-m-b-o-k."

"Got it. I've heard about that place. There was lots going on there, a few years ago, if my addled brain serves me right."

"Yes, we were there during a tumultuous time. There were the terrorist bombings in Bali, and rioting—for various reasons. The economy took a tumble. The East Timor issue, too. The government was toppled not long after my mother and I left—"

"Wait a minute." The woman peered at Naomi through her glasses. "Wait a minute," she whispered, as she continued to stare at Naomi. She then leaned forward and pressed the button to shut off her tape recorder. "You weren't on that...plane, were you? You know the one I mean; there was a plane, a plane filled with people—all sorts of people—that landed somewhere in northern Australia. It was like, some sort of daring escape—"

Naomi nodded.

"That was...you? What did they call it? They called it...*Lombok Freedom Flight*. You were one of the people on that plane?"

Naomi smiled a little at the surprised woman seated across from her. "I don't think I ever heard it called that. Although, when I read about everything that happened later, it was sometimes referred to as *The Mataram Incident.*" Naomi watched the woman reach forward to turn her tape recorder back on.

"Tell me about the, um, incident."

"Well, we managed to get as far as Broome, on what Mike, the pilot, called the smell of a gas rag," said Naomi slowly. "But, you know, it was not just about us, the people in the plane—"

"How many of you were on that plane?"

"There were 48 of us…a world record for a Twin Otter, I think…although we weren't trying for any records."

"Who….were all those people, anyway?"

"Mostly the families of peasants from the area. There were some Chinese families. A Norwegian couple, too. They were tourists who got out. And us."

"Weren't there any students? I thought there were students."

"No…well, yes, there was one…I mean, there were some students killed in Mataram that day, during the demonstration, and many farmers, too. Because there was terrible rioting in the city. But I didn't know any of that was going on at the time."

"They should have known better. Protesting students always get shot at, it seems," the woman replied. "What happened to everyone?"

"From the plane? Well, a few of the women and children live in Australia now, after spending a long time in Nauru, at a refugee camp. Some returned to Indonesia."

"Did you have any friends there?"

"I'm still in touch with some of them. Our friends, the Wayuni family…the mother returned to Lombok. Her two children are in their mid-teens now. In fact, they are going to spend the summer in Manitoba, with my mother."

"Wow, I can't think of a better place to spend a summer. I'm from Minnesota myself." The woman wrote something in her notebook. She looked up at Naomi, and for several moments she did not speak. "I'm sorry…I don't remember the details…I remember reading about the plane, mostly—and all those people killed in the city. Did…was…your father killed?"

"Yes. He died that day…That's what the investigation concluded."

There was another silence, and then Naomi reached behind her and picked a photo off the shelf. "This is my father, Steve. And next to him is Wahab Wayuni. They worked together."

The woman stared at the photo, then shook her head. "You probably hate that country now."

Naomi smiled. "Actually, I'm going back soon."

"Oh…to help with the tsunami…you know…clean up?'"

"That's right. I'm going to Banda Aceh, though. Not Lombok. I've been seconded to the World Food Program. I speak *bahasa*, and I asked to join the tsunami relief mission there. My boss thought it would be good to for me to get some field experience. It'll help my work here; we have several programs in Indonesia. And no doubt we'll be adding a few more there, now."

The woman nodded sympathetically. "I know what you mean. Those poor homeless people. What a tragedy. The tsunami…And so you should. Why would you ever want to go back to that other place, anyway, where your life was…ruined?"

"No, my life wasn't ruined. I don't hate Lombok—and I'm not afraid of it. I'm going to go back there someday."

The woman took the photo from Naomi's hands. "Who's the boy? He's got a nice smile."

"His name is Noor. Wahab's son…my friend."

The woman returned the photo. Naomi held it in her hands for a moment, looking, as she often did, at their smiling faces.

"Whatever happened to the pilot?"

Naomi looked up, "Mike? He's back in Australia. Brisbane. He's settled down. Has a wife and a baby boy. He's happy. I'll be visiting them after my posting to Indonesia is finished."

The woman nodded, writing in her notebook. "Wow. You're quite an inspiration, Naomi. And only 22 years old." She looked up at Naomi and rested her hands in her lap. "What makes you the way you are? I tell you, if it were me, I'd never go back."

"Well… I want to help…Have you ever been to Indonesia, Donna?"

"No. But I hear that Bali is very beautiful, and the people there are so friendly." She hesitated. "What about your mother?"

Naomi's eyes darkened a little. "She's back in Manitoba. I know she likes Indonesia, too, but I don't think she'll ever go back there."

"You said you're leaving soon. You're very brave."

"Everybody says that. My grandparents. My friends. Even my co-workers here. But…I don't know." Naomi stopped, She wanted to choose her words carefully now. She wanted to be understood. "I think…maybe…it's just an ordinary courage. The kind in all of us." Naomi looked again at the photo in her hands, at the three men she had loved, when she was 18 years old.

"So tell me, what happened when you left Lombok and the government toppled? You know, some people say it was your Mataram Incident that was the straw breaking the camel's back for the president there. Kind of like People Power—Indonesian-style."

"Yes, so they say…but it was a long time coming," replied Naomi.

"Naomi I still say you're very brave. Actually, this is turning into another story. A different story altogether. Let's backtrack again, if you don't mind. What happened after you escaped from Lombok?"

Naomi let out a deep breath. "Well, we landed in Broome. And the press was there. We didn't get a chance to spend too much time together. Our friends were sent to Nauru after a day or two. That was awful. My mother and I went to Singapore and we stayed there until we learned what had happened to my dad…then my mom and I returned to Canada. I started university…that had been the plan all along…business administration. But I transferred to a different university to study *bahasa Indonesia* and agricultural economics. I applied for a summer intern job here at the UN, and, I guess, they liked my work."

"Good for you."

"Thanks. So I thought, I'd like to give back to the world…add my light to the sum of lights, if you know what I mean. I think I always knew I'd be back in Indonesia. I believe that a better life is possible there, and should be achieved."

"Your mother must be very proud."

"She is."

"Well thank you, Naomi. What a story. I may even try to sell it to the wire service, or something. Can I take your photo? How about holding your backpack. Your face may end up on the front page of the paper in Port...what did you call it?"

"Portage la Prairie."

"Yeah, that's it. Thanks Naomi. Thanks for the story." The woman rose and Naomi led her back to the door. She put on her poncho then thrust out her hand to Naomi. "I still don't know how you can go back there, after what happened to you."

Naomi didn't know how she could respond. It would take too long. How could she ever explain that the country called to her; that there was a part of her that had never left Indonesia. That she *had* to go back. How could she ever explain to this woman any of that.

Naomi shrugged. "I know what you're saying. But it's not hard for me. I think it's important to try to always better ourselves." Naomi paused for a moment. "It's my most excellent *jihad*, I guess: the one in my soul." She giggled.

The woman looked up from her handbag and stared at Naomi. "Uh...mind if I *don't* quote you on that? Sounds inflammatory. But thanks for your time."

Naomi shrugged, trying to cover up the embarrassment she was feeling for not being understood, yet again. And she suddenly felt very tired, too. She had been thinking about asking the woman for a copy of the story she was writing, but then changed her mind. "My pleasure."

Naomi shut the door behind the woman and returned to her desk. Again, she picked up the photo of Steve, Noor, and Wahab and stared at it for a long time. She would always remember their passion. The one lasting image of the three men would be this one, together at the summit of Mount Rinjani. And their smiles. Naomi smiled back.

She knew Steve and Noor and Wahab were proud of her, cheering her on. Naomi looked into their faces: *How do you ever really know if you would give your life to help others live? Every day, everywhere, ordinary people are put into that situation. Perhaps you are the lucky ones...You know the truth...*

Naomi carefully placed the photo back on her desk and turned to her backpack on the bed. It was time to get ready. She would leave in the morning; Dale was going to drive her to the airport. Already Naomi was starting to get that excited feeling she got when something new was going to happen. Naomi knew she wouldn't get much sleep that night. But she didn't mind; she would sleep on the plane tomorrow. After all, how could anyone sleep when they were teetering on the brink of a new adventure— and a whole new life.

This is the last part in a trilogy about Naomi Nazarevich, a young Canadian who grows up and discovers herself as she discovers the world around her. If you are one of the growing number of young "third-culture kids" living their lives as a citizen of the world, or if you are living in one place but desire and endeavour to understand the issues and cultures of faraway places, I wrote this with you in mind. I hope it will inspire you to see your life as a world without borders.

I would like to acknowledge the input of all the "third-culture kids" I have spoken with over the years, especially those in Hong Kong, who have shared with me their experiences and feelings as a young person growing up globally. I want to thank my homestay family in Yogyakarta, Indonesia, who invited me into their home and introduced me to their Muslim faith with open arms. The memories of my experience in Indonesia, as part of their family, motivated me to write this story. To Ron and Budi, Vera, Victoria, April, and all those who read parts of the manuscript, I am grateful for your comments and suggestions.

Finally, to D. P., Emelyn, Emi, and Blaise: Naomi has grown up— I think we're going to miss her.

—*Karmel Schreyer*

BIBLIOGRAPHY:

Naomi recommends these books about Indonesia:

In the Time of Madness, Richard Lloyd Parry, Jonathan Cape, 2005

Letters of a Javanese Princess, Raden Adjeng Kartini, translated by
   Agnes Louise Symmers, University of America Press, 1985

The Girl from the Coast, Pramoedya Ananta Toer, Hyperion, 2002

The Year of Living Dangerously, Christopher J. Koch,
   Penguin Books, 1978